To Aaradhya, my first and foremost priority.
To Vansh, the invisible thread that always kept us tied.
To Shivani, the comfort in my turmoil.

And to you, dear readers, I hope you find a reflection of yourself between these pages. May this story remind you that love, loss, and learning are all part of growing up.

A Beginning She Never Believed In

It was a new moon that night. The clouds had smothered the sky and rain kept falling—carved out by thunder and rage, as if the storm itself carried a warning. 'Why did we have to meet in the rain?' It ran wild in my head as I stood in front of her. She, for sure, was shorter than me—but the anger on her face felt larger than anything else. Even in the storm, her beauty drew me in—but there was something in her expression, in the way she held herself, that warned me: she could erupt any second, and I couldn't understand what I'd done wrong. *'Kya hua? aise mausam mein achanak se milne ko bula liya?'* I asked.

She shot back angrily, *'Mujhse kya puch raha hai?* Ask yourself.' Ask Myself? About what?

She let out a sigh, shifting to a despairing tone, she said, 'Was I not enough for you?' I was stunned. Why was she saying this? After a pause, she continued, 'Seriously, tell me—what

did I do wrong? Why did you need someone else when you had me?' It felt too vague, I'd never done something like that. I shot back quickly, 'What? Someone else? Who?' To which she angrily replied, 'Don't try to act innocent now, Vansh had told me everything… I had warned you many times, but still you did it.' Vansh? Why would he say that? In his Anger? And what did he say? The memory of him at the escalator in the mall hit me. But to placate her I said, 'He might've said something, but believe me–'
But before I could even finish, she cut me off in the middle, yelling loudly over me, **'I don't believe you!'**
Her words hit me like a punch to the gut. After everything we'd been through, after every late night conversation, every quiet promise… she looked at me like I was a mistake she should've avoided. And I hadn't even done anything. I wanted to fight for it—to say look at me, listen to me, this isn't who I am. But my voice stuck somewhere in my throat, tangled in disbelief and hurt. Because what could you say to someone who's already decided you're not worth trusting?

Her eyes lowered, in a despondent tone, she said, 'Trust is fragile. You build it piece by piece… and then one moment is enough to shatter it… Maybe I wasn't able to be the person who you wanted me to be. *If you love someone, you can hurt others for them!* But maybe it's just one sided, what you felt for me—it was like love but love can't be like this…' Her words settled like ash. Not fire—no heat left—just the

She turned her gaze away and spoke again, quieter this time, like she was talking more to herself than to me, 'I always feared this... that getting close would only make it easier to be let down, as the saying was... *Familiarity breeds contempt*. It does,' she let out a sigh and continued, 'I should've listened to that voice back then—the one that warned me not to trust comfort.'

That line cut deeper than I expected from the last time she used it. She was saying all this like it was the truth. Like I proved her right. I never did what she thought I did. I was just standing there, listening—letting her words sink in. But then I felt a tear slipping from my left eye. She was surprised—like she hadn't expected me to break. But I couldn't take it. Not the weight of being misunderstood. Without saying anything, I ran into the rain. As if I could outrun her doubts—her version of me.

Tears were streaming down my face and they blurred my vision, but no one could tell—because the sky was crying too.
No sooner did I reach home than I rushed inside, making sure no one saw my tear-streaked face. I went straight to my room and locked the door. The air from the AC hit my skin, but it didn't make me feel any lighter. I sank into my chair and let it spin—slow, and aimless, just like my thoughts.
I grabbed my diary. The one place I never had to explain myself. I flipped past the last entry, took a blank page and

started to write. Not to make sense of it—just to get it out. Whatever this feeling was, it had to go somewhere. And when words failed to form full sentences, they came out in fragments—in rhythm, in rhyme. In pain disguised as poetry.

I didn't know what I was doing, only that I needed to bleed, but quietly. So I lifted the pen, wiped the tears from my face, and began:

'Inn khamoshi mai nhi, mai inn jhute aaropon mein kho gaya...

Meri aur meri begunahi ke bich bas ek sacchai ka fasla reh gya!

Abb na jine ka sahas hai aur na marne ka gam

Sath chodna hi tha to jhute sapne kyu dikhaye ki ek sath rahenge hum..

Jo darawana khwaab tha mera ab vo Haqeeqat ban gaya...

Usne kaha chupp, aur mai chup reh gya!'

And with that final line, I let out a sigh. It almost felt strange—how I managed to write shayaris at all. It had been so long since I'd used those words, those carefully woven lines. Why did I even turn to shayari now? The question lingered in my mind for a second before it hit me: it was the only way I knew to channel the storm in my chest. I had learned this from someone I thought would never leave—someone who was now a ghost in my life, their betrayal still fresh. I let out another sigh, almost bitter this time, 'Why did he have to plant something false in her

mind?' The anger, confusion, and hurt pressed down on me.
I couldn't talk it out with anyone.

 I didn't know what to do with myself anymore. So, I wrote.
And as I wrote, something else surfaced. The memories
scribbled inside this diary engulfed me, starting from a day
when I decided I couldn't just sit here letting life happen to
me anymore. It was the early, ailing month of September.
The first-term exams had just concluded, and the date for
the results was finally here. None of us knew then—how
much everything would change because of that day. Not just
because of the marks. But because of what came after.

When It All Set Off

Well, that day was something most students are afraid of. Parent-teacher meetings. Strangely, I wasn't—at least not usually, I mean I'd grown way more careless than your average 11th grader. But somehow, as I sat there with my parents in front of my class teacher, my heart thudded harder than ever. Head low, pretending to be ashamed, I couldn't help but smirk slightly—just enough to stay invisible. Maybe it was the absurdity of the moment or a defense mechanism. But that sheet of paper with my poor results lying openly on the table? That was very real.

I could feel the heat radiating from my mother. She didn't say a word—but her stare burned through me. The kind of stare that didn't need translation. As if she was saying, '*Ghar chal, beta... tujhe batati hoon*.' And yeah... I knew what that meant. We didn't even make it home before it started raining on me, *'kyu... Bada udd raha tha na? Padhne ki jarurat nahi hai... Tujhe to maths mein sab kuch aata tha fir kya hua?* Are we mad that we keep encouraging you to study, we are your parents, we have seen more life than you, don't think like we don't know anything... We are not lecturing, it's for your own good.' I was silent, and grinning, until she said something that hit my head, *'aaj mehnat karoge toh kal ko sab kuch theek rahega. Naukri rahegi, paisa rahega, tumhare hi biwi-bacche khush rahenge... hamara kya rakha hai isme?'*

Mummy was like a never-ending playlist—only instead of music, it was a nonstop mix of taunts, scoldings, and emotional blackmail. And not just that day. She had always been like that, really. But for some reason, her words didn't just land—they lodged, somewhere deeper than I expected.

Maybe it was the way her voice cracked between anger and disappointment or maybe it was the weight of my own silence. But something hit me differently. For the first time, it felt like—maybe they were right. Maybe all those rebukes weren't just noise. Maybe I really was wasting something. And for a moment, a strange guilt wrapped itself around me, whispering that I should stop resisting, that I should just listen to them.

So, that day, I don't really know how, but I decided to study hard—to meet their expectations in the next assessment examination, to bring a smile to their faces. And it wasn't something I was doing half-heartedly. It was real, I meant it.

But *life doesn't keep rewarding obedience for so long*. Just when I'd finally decided to play by their rules... she walked in, and rewrote mine.

Random Manifestation

The days were passing, everything was going well. I was studying properly, and those taunts at home were on the verge of disappearing. I had promised myself to keep maintaining this flow—'This time, I'm gonna top!'

As September ended, my birth month arrived—and I was still in the flow. I was managing everything—my studies, my hobbies, my friends... even my growing obsession with her. But all in limits. I kept control. I never tried approaching her. Not because I didn't want to—but because I was afraid that if I got into all this, I'd slip back into becoming the person I used to be. And to be honest, I didn't even know how to approach her. She was my first love. The first time I ever felt this way, I wasn't familiar with how all these things worked. So, I chose to stay quiet. I told myself—**'If it's meant to happen, it'll happen**.' And until it happens, I just have to keep pushing forward, focused on one thing that is improving my academics.

Then—just two days before my birthday, on 14th October, I was having a usual late-night conversation with Vansh or my so-called best friend on Instagram.

By then, he already knew about my crush on Aaradhya. So, as always, I was just casually wishing things out loud, saying stuff like, 'How nice would it be if she approached me first?' Just random, hopeless romantic thoughts. *The kind you laugh off... but secretly hope for.*
And then came a reply I wasn't ready for. 'I'll do it,' he typed. At first, I didn't even react. I just stared at the screen. I read the words again, just to be sure I hadn't misunderstood. What was he talking about? Did he mean he'd actually go talk to her?
I quickly typed back, 'What do you mean?'
He replied almost instantly—'*Bas dekhte ja.*'
Something about that message felt wrong but exciting. It was so vague, yet somehow felt serious. I couldn't tell if he was joking or if something was actually going on behind the scenes.
My thoughts started spiraling. A part of me was excited, another part was anxious, and a third part just didn't know how to feel. I asked him again what he meant, hoping he'd explain. But that was it. No more replies. Maybe he dozed off. But, did he really mean what he said? And in that silence, my mind started imagining everything that could possibly go wrong.

It was getting a bit too much. My head was full of different sorts of thoughts, so I typed out a few more questions—even though I knew the replies wouldn't come. I was tired of typing that much, so I turned off my phone, placed it on the table, and went to sleep only to see this waiting for me, *'Kya karega jan kar, kam to mujhe karna hai..*
Tu bas ishara kar, mai karunga kyuki mujhe tujhe khush karna hai..'

The next day at school, I bombarded him with questions the moment I saw him. 'What will you do? Or what did you do?'
To which, he just smiled and said, 'Talk to her.'
Which made me even more restless, questioning him throughout the day, 'What did she say?' and 'Are you sure you can actually do it?' But all he gave me was, *'Sahi waqt ke aane par jaan ne se sabhi baatein suhani lagegi...*
Bharosa kar mujhpar aur mere tariko par, tujhe teri ye kahani behtareen lagne lagegi...'
That line—so vague, so calm—felt like torture. It was like when you know someone is planning a birthday surprise for you, and you're dying to figure it out. You keep throwing hints, asking around, hoping someone slips up. But no one says anything. It was exactly that feeling—something exciting is definitely about to happen, but no one's telling you how, when, or what. And it keeps eating you alive from the inside.

Even before we parted ways from school, I tried asking him one last time—but he just smiled and stayed quiet.

No sooner did I reach home, I rushed to Instagram and texted him again. But there too, he kept ignoring all my questions, dodging them like they didn't even exist. Finally, after a lot of urging—practically begging, to at least inform me when this was going to happen, to which he replied with just two words, 'Maybe tomorrow.'
Tomorrow? A shock of excitement hit me—on my birthday? So it was really like a birthday surprise coming my way. 'OMG tomorrow? Thank you!' I texted him back, already grinning like an idiot.
But then he replied with, 'Don't be so happy, I said maybe.' My jaw dropped, total mood-killer, he really knew how to mess up with me.

Still, I couldn't help it. I couldn't focus on anything else. Without realizing it, I'd skipped studying. My rhythm, my discipline—completely derailed. But in that weird, happy haze, the day passed. And then, it was there—16th October, My birthday.

I got a lot of wishes. When I checked WhatsApp—there were just a few 12 a.m. wishes, including one from Vansh. I regretted sleeping early, I missed out the midnight vibe. But then again, I was okay with it but still curious about the forthcoming surprise. I texted Vansh again, '*At least birthday ke din toh bata de.*'

To which he replied, '*Surprise batate nahi, thoda toh sabr rakh.*'

I let out a sigh and agreed, trying to calm my racing thoughts. Before leaving the chat, I asked him just one last thing—'*At least itna bata de, sab theek toh jaa raha hai na?*' My message stayed delivered but unseen—he had gone offline. No reply, no blue ticks. So, I moved on with my birthday.

In the morning, I visited the temple and simply came back home, the usual small celebrations, though we were going out for dinner later that night. But the entire day passed—no updates from him, no surprise, nothing. By late evening, my excitement had quietly settled into a dull acceptance. Maybe it wasn't happening after all. But I kept checking my phone regularly.

While getting ready for dinner, my phone buzzed, it was our class WhatsApp group. Tons of birthday wishes were flooding in. I scrolled through them, but my eyes were only searching for one name. But it was absent. Disappointed, I typed a quick, 'Thank you all,' looked at the time—7:23 PM it was. I was just about to turn off the phone when—
A Snapchat notification popped up on my screen

'Aaradhya<3! sent a chat.'

Heart Skipped A Beat

I clicked the floating notification with a kind of urgency that made it feel like if I was even a second late, the moment would slip right through my fingers. My screen froze for a bit—of course it would, what else can you expect from a phone surviving on 4GB RAM? I stomped my foot in frustration, silently begging it to load and just when I thought the suspense would kill me, it finally did load. There it was, 'happy birthday Anuj.' Simple. But it hit like an electrifying storm. My heart swelled with something I couldn't put into words—a wave of joy, maybe even hope... *that strange, addictive kind of happiness only your first love can bring.*

I was about to send a 'thank you,' when another message popped up. 'I want to tell you something.'
My heart thudded—loud, wild, unbearable. For a second, I forgot to breathe. Hope sparked before I could even control it. I deleted the 'thank you' without a second thought. Something Vansh said earlier buzzed in my mind. Was this that moment?

I quickly typed, 'Even I want to say something... *par mujhse nahi bola jayega. Pehle tu bol.*' She replied almost instantly, 'How will I, if you aren't able to?' with an innocent faced emoji. *'Bas... bata na,'* I sent. 'Hmm.' And then... She started typing. For so long, I watched those three dots above her bitmoji blink, vanish, and return—until finally, her message came through, 'I don't know when it started exactly... There wasn't a big moment or some dramatic reason. It just kept growing quietly, every single day. You'd laugh at something, and I'd find myself smiling. You'd answer in class, and I'd listen even if I wasn't paying attention before. I didn't plan to feel anything, I swear. It just happened. And I never said anything because there was no reason for you to even notice me, let alone feel the same. But when Vansh told me you might like me too... something in me said, 'maybe'. Just maybe, this isn't all one-sided. And if there's even a small chance—then I had to take it. So here I am... just saying it: I love you. A lot. More than I ever expected to. And if this messes everything up, I'll live with that. But I didn't want to keep it to myself anymore.'
My eyes widened. My breath caught in my throat. It felt like time had just frozen. I read the message again. Once. Twice. Thrice. As if my brain needed confirmation that I wasn't imagining this. That she had actually said it.
'I—I can't believe you love me?' I typed, stunned. But even in that moment of joy, doubt crept in—quiet but persistent. I had a strange feeling. What if Vansh had forced her to just say it for my happiness? Just like he always tried to pull

strings. So I asked, 'Are you sure about it? Or did Vansh somehow push you into saying this?'
She replied almost instantly, 'I'm sure about it! I've been secretly loving you for a long time, but I didn't confess because I was scared. Scared you wouldn't feel the same. And even if you did, there was something else I was afraid of. But the moment Vansh told me about your feelings... I thought maybe it's now or never.'
My heart felt like it had been kissed by heaven. Her words wrapped around me like warmth on a cold day.
But still, something didn't sit right. 'What was that other thing you were afraid of?' I typed, unable to resist asking. My curiosity overpowered the excitement. Her typing bitmoji popped up again. Then vanished. Then came back. 'It was... Uhm... I don't know how to explain...' But she stopped midway. Nothing more came.

Frustrated, I tossed and turned on my bed so hard that my phone slipped from my hands. For a second, I felt my soul leave my body. But it landed safely on the mattress. I grabbed it, quickly, almost desperate to not miss another word. And there it was—her reply, sitting heavy on my screen, *'You know they say—Familiarity breeds contempt.'*
My fingers hovered over the keyboard for a few seconds. That line—'Familiarity breeds contempt'—hit harder than I thought it would. I knew what she meant, what she feared. That one day, the closeness might turn into carelessness. That love might dissolve into indifference. And the fact that

she felt the need to say that... It hurts. But I couldn't let her sit with that fear. Not even for a second. 'Aaradhya,' I typed, my hands slightly trembling, 'I know why you're saying this. And I won't give you some perfect line to prove otherwise. But please know this—I'm not here to get bored, to forget, or to stop choosing you. I'm not like that. I never will be.' I paused, then added, 'You don't have to believe in forever right now. Just believe in this—I'm not going anywhere. But... If you did it.' I took another pause before sending in, 'then nothing, because *I love you, come to me and I'll surely forgive you every time.*'

A Missing Change

And yeah, my commitment was true...

The chat continued for several minutes, each message a tiny thread weaving me deeper into a web of excitement I couldn't escape. Even during dinner, I kept checking my phone, sneaking peeks between bites. It was only when I finally lay down in bed, still clutching the device like it held my entire universe, that I allowed myself to breathe.
That night—no, that birthday—was the best one of my life. It brought me happiness... but along with that, it brought something else too—*Change*.
The next morning, we saw each other for the first time since those chats. On the school bus.
Our homes were barely a kilometre apart, so we shared the same bus. But today, something felt different. The moment the bus arrived, I got in with only one thought in mind—her. She was already there, sitting with Aarohi, deep in conversation. But when our eyes met, time seemed to freeze.

For a second, we just stared at each other. And then—just
like that—we both looked away, blushing. It was as if
everything that had been so natural between us before
suddenly felt new.

I quietly took the seat behind hers, next to Ashwin. But I
couldn't stop myself from glancing at the back of her head,
like an idiot. Something had shifted between us—we'd never
been this shy.

Ashwin nudged me, his voice low. 'You okay? Why are you
staring at her like that?'

How could I explain it? How could I tell him that
everything was different now? That she had just admitted to
loving me—something I'd never thought possible?

At school, it was no better. Passing each other between
classes, our eyes would meet for a split second before we'd
both quickly look away, our faces warming with
embarrassment. We'd smile shyly but didn't know how to
speak.

Every time I tried to start a conversation, the weight of last
night's words would come crashing down on me. The
intensity of it all—the love, the fear, the hope—was too
much to handle. It felt too real, too big. And neither of us
seemed prepared for it.

We weren't avoiding each other. We just… didn't know how
to be 'us' yet. Not in this new space we found ourselves in.

But everything had *changed*.

Something Grateful To Have

Vansh was already grinning by the time I approached. *'Kaisa raha?'* he asked, that familiar mischief glowing on his face. I couldn't hold back my blushing. It just... happened.
As I slid into the seat next to him, he leaned in, eager for the full story. I wasn't going to hide anything from him but still I glanced at Aaradhya and she was already looking at me—like she knew this moment was coming. I lifted a finger and pointed at Vansh. She gave a small nod, a soft smile on her face. Permission granted.

So, I told him everything. And God, I was thankful to him. Really. If he hadn't said what he did to her, maybe none of this would've happened. He just smiled quietly as I spoke, like he already knew it would play out this way.

Unfortunately, though, the school day passed without a single real conversation between me and Aaradhya. Just one small sign—but it meant something. Still, it was hard, seeing her and not being able to talk like we used to. Or maybe, like we were supposed to now.

But once we were back home... things shifted.

On Snapchat, the awkwardness disappeared. It was like the chats were our real world now, and talking face-to-face was the dream we hadn't learned how to exist in together yet.

That evening, as I lay scrolling through chats, her name popped up again. 'It felt kinda weird today, didn't it?' she wrote.

I couldn't help but smile. I told her I had tried to speak to her so many times in school, but the words just never made it out.

'I know,' she replied. 'I don't know why it felt so awkward suddenly.' Maybe it was because we'd never shared something like that before, and now that it was out there, everything felt more real—maybe too real.

She added, 'I thought after the confession, things would feel easier. But it's the opposite.'

I agreed. Every time I looked at her in school, I wanted to say something. Anything. But I just froze. I told her how my brain would stop working the moment our eyes met.

'I noticed,' she said. 'I did the same. And the way we looked away and smiled like idiots...'

I chuckled, typing, 'Yeah... I really wanted to hear your voice.'

'I wanted to hear yours too,' she replied softly. 'It's crazy how we talk so much here but go completely quiet in person.' I told her maybe we just needed a little time. 'We'll get there,' I assured. 'I don't want us to stay stuck in silence.' She didn't take long to respond. 'Me neither. We'll figure it out... slowly.'

An Unfiltered Bond

We tried... We really did. But no matter how much we chatted, how many sweet messages were exchanged under starry nights, it just wouldn't get any better in real life. The awkwardness stuck like a wall between us—until one day in November.

Few days earlier than that day, Vansh had come over to my house. We had a group assignment due, and since we both lived nearby, it made sense to work together. Mummy, as always, couldn't help but hover around. She kept throwing questions at him like she was taking an entrance interview. I cringed inside—why did she have to test him?

But what I didn't see coming was what happened next.

When I asked Vansh to pass me a pen from the table, he stumbled into the curtain covering my bookshelf. It slipped off, revealing my entire collection—rows of books stacked unevenly, some bent at the corners, but all deeply loved.

He stared like he'd just uncovered some hidden world. 'Whoa, whose books are all these?' he asked. 'Mine,' I said, a little amused. His expression shifted to shock.

'I didn't know you studied this much!' I laughed. 'Study? Me? No, these are all novels.'

He looked reassured, but a beat later his brows furrowed again. 'You once said you had only a few, and that no one even buys you more. Then how come... this whole lot?'

I smirked and shrugged. 'I didn't lie. No one bought me these books. I bought these myself. Offers, sales—I saved up every bit of money I could. Birthday cash, those ₹50-₹100 notes from relatives back in the village... it adds up.'

He just said one word—'Dedication.'

I murmured back, 'Yeah... dedication, and a lot of struggle. But it helped. Helped me see how this world really works.'

'How?' he asked. I looked at him, a little lost in thought, and said, 'I realized something... That **nothing is truly yours in this cursed world. If you want something—Don't beg for it. Snatch it.**'

Silence followed. Not awkward. Just... heavy.

I pulled the curtain back over the shelves. He stood, wandered toward the bookshelf, scanning the spines like he was looking for something.

'Do you want a book?' I asked.

He turned back, waving a hand. 'No, no. I'm not into this wholesome stuff.'

'Shut up! At least it's better than your cartoons—or what do you call it? Yeah, anime,' I shot back
We argued a bit, laughed a bit more. Then silence returned. But this time, in that quiet, the thing that had been bothering me for days lit up again in my mind. That urge to finally say it—to finally tell him what was weighing on me...

I talked to him about Aaradhya. About how we were so good over chat, yet in person we turned into strangers, how regret had started to take root in the pauses between stolen glances and missed chances. He listened, nodding, looking thoughtful. Then, he offered a few possible reasons—maybe it was fear. Fear of publicity, of drawing attention we weren't ready for. 'Ignore it,' he said gently, 'You'll have to.' Maybe he was right. Maybe that fear was real. But we couldn't just ignore—it could have been a trouble maker. But then he added something more, something he always did—hope.

'I'll handle it,' he smiled, confident like always. 'I'll make sure you both get the time, the moments. Just wait, you'll talk soon.'

And once again, he left me on a cliffhanger. He didn't tell me what he was planning. Just that look on his face—the one that always meant trouble or something brilliant. But I hoped for it.

The First Step

And this time, I didn't have to regret it.

That day in November was different. I simply got into the bus and took my usual spot behind her, just like every other day. I was sitting there—unbothered, unsuspecting, but I was completely unaware of what was coming next.
And then it happened.

She turned back, looked at me for a second, and said—*'Kaise yaar... Itna chup kyu baitha rehta hai...'* I was caught so off-guard, I blinked twice before I could even react.
She laughed softly, then added, *'kuch to bol, online to bahut bolta hai! Yaha kya ho jata hai.'* For a second, I just stared, trying to register that she actually spoke. And somehow, I managed to say, *'kya bolu mai,'* and blushed.
She rolled her eyes but smiled again, this time brighter.

Then came a small pause, not awkward, just... quiet. The kind that sits comfortably between people trying. She didn't turn back immediately, just kept half-facing me and said, *'Ajeeb lag raha hai kya?'* I nodded, *'Haan, thoda.'*

She chuckled under her breath and I smiled back. For a
moment it felt like nothing more was needed.
She turned back to face ahead, but that moment stayed with
me—the first step. A tiny one, maybe, but enough to melt
whatever wall had been standing between us all this while.

The silence after that wasn't heavy anymore. It had shifted
into something lighter and warmer, though it felt a little bit
weird, but I believed we could gradually enhance it.

When we reached school, I hadn't even stepped off the bus
properly when Vansh caught up with me. The moment he
looked at my face, he knew something had happened. I gave
a small nod to confirm it—we did talk, briefly.

But when I admitted that I couldn't say much back, that I
had just stayed quiet, his expression changed. He didn't need
to say much; his reaction said it all. The disappointment, the
urgency, the frustration—it all landed like a punch.
According to him, she must've gathered a lot of courage to
speak first, and I had let that moment slip.

And as he walked off shaking his head, I stood there still.
The guilt crept in like a slow chill. I hadn't just been
quiet—I had failed to acknowledge her effort. And now, I
had to make it right somehow. But how!?

I spent the rest of the day scanning for a moment—any moment—to speak to her again. I'd messed up earlier, and the weight of it was pressing hard. But no matter how much I tried, I couldn't find the right time, the right excuse. It was like the day was slipping away too quickly, and I was running behind it, empty-handed.

Then, sometime post-lunch, I was loitering near the staff room corridor with Vansh, Aarohi, and a few girls. We were just killing time when Ms. Vidya, our class teacher, spotted us and asked if someone could go call Aaradhya. That was it. That was my moment. But before I could react, the girls took the cue and began walking ahead.

It felt like the opportunity was being snatched right from under me. I leaned into Vansh and whispered that I wanted to do it—I needed to. He looked at me, half-surprised, half-amused, and chuckled. I pleaded, almost shamelessly, and he finally gave in.
With his signature storytelling flair, he ran to intercept the girls, spinning something up just like he always did. He had a knack for that kind of thing—talking his way through anything, especially with girls. A total charmer, but more importantly that day—my lifesaver.

I took off in the other direction, heart thudding, and found Aaradhya. I hesitated for a moment, then managed a small smile and told her softly that ma'am was calling her. At first, she looked unaffected, but then—she smiled back. Not a big one, just enough. She nodded and started walking, and I followed a few steps behind, floating in a moment that felt golden, unreal.

As we neared the staffroom, the rest of our group caught up. Aarohi, loud as always, said, 'Vidya miss *bula rahi hai.*' Without breaking stride, Aaradhya replied, *'Haan, Anuj ne bata diya tha.'*

And just like that, she acknowledged me—in front of them. She didn't need to. But she did. And in that second, I felt this strange, overwhelming mix of pride and happiness burst inside me. I actually jumped a little where I stood, and smiled like an idiot.

Because **when you're in love, even the smallest sign feels like heaven.**

I've always looked for those signs that I chased her to a point I awaited from my very first step. We had been following this rhythm for a while now—slow, steady, almost like we were finding our way through a fog. Each conversation, no matter how small, had slowly chipped away at the barrier that had kept us apart. It wasn't instant, but gradually, the awkwardness eased. We tried, little by little, exchanging the simplest words we could muster. And somewhere along the way, it all started to come together.

And eventually, we found ourselves talking without hesitation—completely, fully.

Between Fireworks And Silence

I was almost living the kind of life any middle-class teen would dream of. Days were passing like a soft breeze—simple, happy, light. I was able to talk to her. Though in-person conversations stayed clear of anything romantic, those reserved spaces belonged to our late-night Snapchat chats. In school, we spoke about the oddest things—silly topics, random jokes—and somehow, those weird conversations wove themselves into our growing bond. It was love, just wrapped in a different cloth. Gradually, we even started having contretemps.

One afternoon, while returning from school, we were talking about chocolates. Aarohi mentioned her love for Ferrero Rocher. I immediately jumped in, claiming it was my favorite too. Aaradhya wrinkled her nose and said, *'Chii, kitna ganda lagta hai vo.* I like Silk more.' Triggered, I couldn't resist mocking, *'Vo sasti chocolate!'* She turned back sharply, her face scrunched in playful irritation. *'Tere Ferrero*

Rocher se to acha hi hai,' she snapped. 'Nice joke,' I shot back.
Her angry glare caught me off-guard, and with a voice just a little louder than needed, she ordered, *'Chup kar.'*
That *'chup kar'* had a weight to it—it really did silence me that day.

It became a pattern. One day we argued about supercars, another day about which teacher taught better, and sometimes we even fought without any memory later of why we started. Once, she was so angry at something I had said that when Ashwin pranked her by tapping her on the head, she turned around and hit me without even checking who had done it. Her behavior was getting rough, but somehow, even in the rudeness, there was something beautiful—a closeness.

During Diwali vacations, something shifted. Maybe because we weren't meeting in person, maybe because words flowed easier behind a screen—but for a few days, it felt like the old closeness had returned.

That night, after dressing up, I sent her a snap—wearing the clothes she had once insisted would look good on me. She reacted with a simple grinning emoji, her Bitmoji peeking shyly from the bottom. But she didn't type anything. No comment, no teasing. I stared at the screen, waiting in the noise of the firecrackers, but nothing dropped

in. Not wanting the silence to stretch, I clicked a quick snap of my new shoes. 'New Shoes. *Kaise hai?*' I captioned. A short, dry reply came—'Nice.'
I couldn't tell what was hiding behind that one word. Before I could ask, her snap arrived. Her shoes too, with exactly the same caption. For a second, I smiled wide. She was playing along. 'Oye! Copycat!' I sent quickly.
'I'm not copying,' she wrote back. 'I had new shoes too, so thought of asking.' And suddenly, the night felt lighter. Then, the snaps came in a flurry—The vibrant swirl of rangolis. The bright crackle of sparklers. The glittering chaos of the festival. And then...
Her.

A picture of her, draped in a sky-blue saree. Elegant and Dreamlike. The soft fall of her hair, the shimmer of her earrings, the brightness of her eyes—I forgot to breathe. It felt like time itself paused to watch her. As I sat frozen, another message popped up. 'Hello?' Still staring, still lost, I didn't reply. *'Kuch bolega bhi?'* she sent again, teasing, pulling me back gently. I typed the only word that made sense at that moment, 'Wow.' She replied with a burst of emojis—a laughing face, a soft smile, hearts spinning—and somewhere in that playful chaos, she slipped something precious.
I picked up a rose from the Diwali decor and sent her a picture. A simple gesture, but my heart was beating too fast.

There was a pause. Then she messaged—*'Ek baat bolu?'* My
heart tightened. I tapped yes. And then it came, small, quiet,
blissing: 'I love you.'
For a second, everything—the world, the noise, the
fireworks outside—blurred into nothingness.
It was just her words, lighting up my sky more than any
firecracker ever could. It was a night carved into my soul.

But like all exceptions, it stayed a moment apart.
After Diwali, when normal life resumed, so did her
roughness—the arguments, the teasing, the playful distance.
And yet, somehow, the glow of that one night stayed
burning quietly inside me.

But I was too frustrated, too unhappy with her behavior.
But I couldn't tell her directly. Every time I thought about
it, the fear crept in—What if I hurt her? What if she thought
I was complaining? So I stayed silent. Swallowed it down.

But somewhere deep inside, I knew I couldn't keep it locked
up forever. I needed her to understand, to feel what I was
feeling. And I knew exactly how to do it—through Vansh.

Finally, one day in the classroom, when I had made up my
mind to talk to him about it, I found him oddly distracted.
He was sitting there, staring absentmindedly toward the
girls' row, somewhere around where Aarohi usually sat. I
called him once, but he didn't respond. I shook him lightly,

and only then he blinked, his face suddenly tensing up as if caught in some inner struggle. Before I could ask anything, he turned to me with a hurried, almost desperate look and said, *'Bhai, ek baat batani hai.'*

Sensing the urgency on his face, I nodded without a second thought. And then he blurted out, as if it had been burning on the tip of his tongue from a long—*'I have a crush on Aarohi!'*

Shared Secrets

For a moment, I simply stared at him, trying to absorb what he had just said. It felt so sudden, so unexpected, that the words I had prepared for him slipped away like sand through my fingers. He looked at me with a strange urgency, his face carrying a rare kind of vulnerability. It was clear he needed support, the way a secret once spoken clings to the listener. And without hesitation, I found myself silently promising him that I would help. His trust was something I couldn't betray, not after everything. My own worries—the frustrations I had bottled up about Aaradhya—faded into the background. They could wait.

For now, it was about him. About standing by him the way he had always stood by me, without questions, without conditions. Even if somewhere deep inside, a small ache reminded me that maybe my own story was going to stay paused a little longer.

I had been carrying enough weight on my shoulders already, but after hearing about Vansh's silent story—his secret feelings for Aarohi hidden away for so long—something inside me shifted. I couldn't turn away from him, not after seeing the look in his eyes that day.

But I couldn't ignore myself either. My own story with Aaradhya was still there, breathing quietly in a corner of my heart, waiting for a moment that kept slipping away. I had barely begun to make sense of what to do when another blow landed—the exam timetable was announced.

It felt like the ground beneath me changed overnight. My decision to study, I have forgotten it all from when it began, and now exams are falling in too.

I didn't know what to do, or even how to begin. I hadn't yet found the courage to speak to Aaradhya about my own feelings—how was I supposed to take charge of someone else's love story?
But then, a memory sparked in my mind: how many times Vansh had helped me without a second thought. Maybe it was my turn now. Drawing from his old tricks, I decided to approach Aaradhya. After all, she and Aarohi were as close as Vansh and I were.

I reached out to her, hinting that there was something important we had to do for Vansh. And then, when the moment felt right, I told her the truth—that Vansh had been quietly in love with Aarohi all this while.

Her reaction, however, wasn't what I expected. She seemed stunned, almost as if she thought I was joking. But once I convinced her it was real, her expression shifted in an instant—a rush of excitement lighting up her face. Only then she shared her own secret: Aarohi had a crush on Vansh too.

We were both taken aback by the coincidence, amazed at how two hearts had been beating quietly for each other all along, but then I realized we were no exception, we also did the same. Without wasting time, we decided we wouldn't let hesitation get in the way. We started planning, little by little, nudging them closer, creating moments without making it obvious. And somehow, almost like a dream unfolding before us, we managed to unite them.

It was obvious that we could make it happen, though it took longer than I had imagined—November was already at the verge of ending by the time everything fell into place. Throughout this whole journey, Aaradhya had stayed her usual, cheerful self. It made me drop the plan of ever bringing up our old quarrels; they had started feeling too small to matter now.

Meanwhile, exams loomed closer, barely a dozen days away. The memory of my promise—made long back during the last exam results—that I would perform better this time, weighed heavily on me. I tried to stay true to it. Tried to focus, tried to pull myself together. But it was hard. Books would open, notes would spread out before me, but my mind... it wandered too easily.
I'd study a little, enough to pretend to myself that I was trying, and then almost unconsciously, my hand would reach for the phone—to text her, to see if she was there.

Mum's rebukes had become a part of my daily routine by then—sharp reminders that I was losing time, that I had promised better. But my heart wasn't ready to listen; it already belonged somewhere else. *Somewhere deep inside Snapchat... it had become our secret place.* A space where no one could reach us, where our words floated free, untouched by the real world.

A few days before exams, I was busy texting her, half pretending to study, when Mum caught sight of me. She stormed into the room. In a flash, I turned off Snapchat, locked the phone, and tossed it aside, pretending to focus on my books. It was my actions only which made her grow suspicious of me. It really feels bad to hide something from our parents but we couldn't afford to be caught. We couldn't even dream of revealing anything—not when the price was certain, scolding, maybe even *separation*. And so,

from those days I started living in the shadow of fear,
pretending everything was normal while inside, everything
had been shaken.

An Uncertain Beginning

She downloaded Instagram for the first time in December, just a couple of days before our midterm exams. And from there, it continued—our quiet, secret world shifting platforms but never losing its warmth. The night before the first paper—Physics—we were chatting late. She had finished her preparations long ago, while I was still flipping through chapters, trying to study some of them for the very first time. In the middle of my anxious scrolling and scribbling, she sent a flying good luck from her screen. And yeah... I really needed it.

After that, she barely came online, and even in school, we hardly got any time to talk. The exams had taken over everything—the air around us, the faces, the conversations. Everything felt muted. But when the exams finally ended, everything slowly came back. The life, the laughter, the ease between us—I was relieved.
Until 21st December, when the results came. And this time, it was even worse than before.

I cried hard that day—unlike the last time. Somewhere deep, I knew I had failed not just on paper, but on the promises I made to myself, to my parents. I really needed to change. I really needed to study for the final examinations.

That night, though I cried a lot, moaned over my mistakes, made all the right promises to myself and to my parents—all to hear, 'we shouldn't have believed you' from them. I wanted to prove them wrong but in the end, I couldn't separate myself from the world I had built, the world that now quietly revolved around Aaradhya.
No matter how urgent the need to focus, how loud the alarms in my head rang—my heart still found its way back to her, every time. **It was like hugging a rose... You were lost in the fragrance while your whole body got pricked by its thorns.**

It hadn't even been a dozen days since I'd sworn to change, yet there I was—drawn back to her like gravity. And why wouldn't I be? It was New Year's Day.
While the world scribbled resolutions in dusty journals, Aaradhya and I were writing the opening lines of a grander chapter—together. 2024 had just begun, and so had we, once again.

On the night of the 31st, I was up on the terrace with my bua's family, waiting for midnight to strike—chasing that 12 a.m. vibe I had missed on my birthday. Me and my cousin were helping prepare *litti-chokha* over the *chulha*, under that cold, festive sky. There was laughter, some harmless teasing, and of course, the most irritating question of all—'What have you thought about your future?' I laughed it off at first, but it kept circling back until I couldn't take it anymore. Maybe I was too blunt, too cold—but I was frustrated that I ignored it. I mean it was the last night of the year. Couldn't we talk about something else, just for once?

Finally, as the chatter settled and the energy fizzled out, everyone lay around drowsily on the terrace. It was just 11:39—and we were barely clinging to consciousness, we were on the verge of dozing off. I didn't even realize when the clock struck twelve. Suddenly, the sky burst into life—fireworks lit every corner of the night. Jolted by adrenaline and that strange New Year's dedication, I stood up. Around me, everyone was asleep, but I managed to capture the moment—a picture of the sky painted with light—and sent it to Aaradhya with a quiet but touching wish.

The sky was beautiful, truly. I stared at it a little longer and whispered to myself, 'If only I had seen this with her.' I hadn't noticed my cousin behind me until he asked, 'With whom?' I froze for a second but managed to mask the truth with a lazy excuse, hoping he'd just go back to sleep. And yeah, he believed me. I wished him, he wished me back, and I led him to the bed. After that, I slipped back upstairs. Everyone else was asleep. I found a quiet corner, pulled out my phone, and opened Instagram—half expecting silence, but there she was. She was awake, 'Happy New Year!' her message read.

And right after it, she replied to my pic— 'I wanted to see the fireworks with you...' I stared at the words. My heart felt full. *'Muh ki baat chheen li,'* I replied. 'Maybe one day...' she typed. Then after a pause—'Still... it's beautiful, right?'
'Yes, it is,' I wrote quickly, 'but what?'
She sent a laughing emoji and then: 'That we got to start 2024 together.'
I don't know why, but that one line stayed with me. I was smiling like an idiot. I typed, 'This year's gonna be the best year!' And then added, 'Just one thing's missing.'
She asked, 'What?'
I replied, 'A glimpse of yours.'
She understood—like always. And within seconds, my phone lit up with her video call. I picked it up with butterflies in my stomach. We didn't say much. We didn't need to. She smiled to which I blushed and looked away. Silence hung softly between us, and somehow it felt more expressive than words ever could.
It hadn't even been five minutes when I noticed movements around—my parents were awake. I quickly ended the call, texted her a hasty explanation, switched off my phone, and curled up like I had been asleep all along. They didn't suspect a thing. Eventually, mom came up to call me down too. I stretched, feigned a yawn, and followed her quietly.

And that's how the year began—with a spark in the sky, a smile on a screen, and a silence that felt like home. A long journey—happy, hectic, and everything in between—was waiting ahead.

The First Morning

We all woke up late. It was a holiday for us—but not for Mum. She was already busy with the household chores. 2024 had begun. It could've been just another day, but our plans didn't let that happen. My friend circle had decided to meet up—to kick off the year together.
After a quick bath, I put on grey trousers and a navy-blue shirt. I styled my hair, then stood in front of the mirror, grinning. *'Kitna handsome hai re tu,'* I said to myself in the mirror. Just then, I heard the honk of an EV outside—Vansh had come to pick me up.
I sprayed some perfume, put on my socks and shoes, and rushed down to him.
'Oh ho, itna saj-dhaj ke kis se milne ja raha hai?' Vansh teased as I climbed onto his Ola electric scooter. I blushed, and he added with a grin, 'Happy New Year, *bhai.'*
I returned the wish, and we set off.
On the way, Vansh looked at me and grinned, *'Oye hoye, aaj toh bhai full set hai! Kya scene hai? New Year ke saath nayi*

shuruat?' I rolled my eyes and smirked, *'Bas bhai, naya saal, nayi trimming.'*

He nudged me with his elbow, *'Nayi trimming nahi, nayi feeling lag rahi hai. Aaradhya ka plan hai kya aaj?'*

I laughed, *'Haan, jaisa tu Aarohi ke saath poetry nights plan karta hai na?'*

Vansh choked on his own laugh, *'Abey chup! Us din toh waise bhi misunderstanding tha.'*

I shook my head, *'Haan haan, sab samajh rahe hain hum... miss wali misunderstanding!'*

He made a face, and we both cracked up. We kept the banter going until we reached the mall. As we rolled into the parking area, to our surprise, the others were already waiting for us there.

'VIPs aa gaye,' Kunal called out, clapping mockingly.

'Traffic mein fas gaye the, bro. Aur kya!' Vansh threw the excuse casually, parking the scooty.

I high-fived a couple of them and we got into our usual mess—punching shoulders, roasting each other's outfits, and debating over where to head first.

Someone suggested the food court, but another was already pulling us toward the arcade.

'Bhookh lag rahi hai, par pehle arcade chalo,' Arun said.

We ended up agreeing on a quick round of games first. Bowling was the obvious choice. The competitive energy kicked in fast—every missed shot became a roast opportunity, and every strike was celebrated like a World

Cup win. I wasn't doing great, but neither was anyone else, so the trash talk kept us all equally humiliated.

After games, we hit the food court—ordered shawarmas and grabbed our seats like we owned the place. No fancy talk, no overthinking—just boys, food, and unfiltered fun. It was loud, messy, and perfect.

We wandered through the mall, floor by floor, not planning to buy anything—just casually roaming. The fourth floor was the fanciest one, full of flashy clothes, designer accessories, gift shops, and oddly enough—a perfume store. We strolled in and started trying different testers, even though deep down we knew we couldn't afford a single bottle. Still, it was fun pretending.

While the others messed around, I lingered at the women's counter. Something had struck me—Aaradhya's birthday was next month. That thought alone pulled me toward the perfumes. It felt strange standing there, unsure, but I tried to keep my cool. Just then, Vansh came jogging over and smirked, *'Uske liye dekh raha hai kya?'*

I scratched my neck, a bit embarrassed, and nodded, *'Birthday aa raha hai na...'*

Vansh let out a dramatic whistle and grinned, *'Aage badh raha hai bhai tu toh!'*

I gave him a playful shove and turned back to the counter. Atif usually had a solid nose for perfumes—I thought about asking him for help, but Vansh said he and the others were at the gaming zone again. So, I was on my own.

As I scanned the premium section, a scent suddenly stopped me in my tracks. It was familiar—warm, sweet, and haunting. I followed it to the bottle: ₹32,000. I stared, not just at the price tag, but at the strange feeling tugging at me. Where had I smelled this before?

I was still trying to piece it together when Vansh returned, a small paper bag in hand.

'Tune bhi kuch le liya?' I asked.

He shrugged with a grin, *'Haan... ek basic combo tha, men-women. Budget mein aa gaya.'*

Lucky him. I, on the other hand, couldn't buy a thing. Nothing felt right. Either it was too expensive or I just couldn't decide. Her birthday was still a month away, but the worry had already set in. What if I picked something wrong?

On our way home, I told Vansh about my dilemma. He laughed and shook his head, *'Tu sach mein pagal ho raha hai. Pura mahina hai abhi!'*

Maybe he was right. But no matter how much I tried, I couldn't shake off that itch—that I needed to find something just right for her.

I came back home around 6:30 PM. Bua had already left. I gave Mum a short version of the day— *'mall gaye the, timepass kiya, thoda perfume dekha'*—just enough to avoid further questions.

After dinner, I lay on the bed, lazily scrolling through Instagram. My stories were flooded—group pics, awkward poses, half-blinked smiles. We'd taken more photos than I remembered. I tapped through each one, pausing whenever I saw myself. *'Accha lag raha hoon,'* I whispered to myself, a small smile playing on my lips.

Then the story flipped—Aarohi had posted something. The girls had met up too.

I tapped quickly, barely noticing the others. I was looking for only one face. And there she was. Aaradhya—In navy blue. My heart actually skipped.

I blinked, stared, swiped back to make sure I wasn't imagining it. It was navy blue—just like me. Coincidence? Maybe. But it didn't feel like one.It felt like a sign. Like we were wired into the same frequency without even trying. Same color. Same day. Same thought, maybe? I couldn't hold it in. I rushed to our chat. She was online. My heart started racing like it always did when I saw that green dot. I didn't even wait—I typed, 'You were in navy blue too??' She replied almost instantly, 'I know right! I saw your story too.' I grinned. *'Yaar,* it's like we matched without even planning.' And then came the message that made my chest feel like it was suddenly too small for my heart—'I was too nervous... I knew you'd see these pics... so I dressed up like this. For you.' For a second, I just stared at the screen, frozen. It wasn't just a *coincidence* anymore. It was something else. Something warm and quiet and unforgettable.

She then said with a smiling emoji, 'Hope it stays like this. Matching, unintentionally.' I didn't know what to say after that. So I just let the silence between messages say it for me. Something had begun. And it was beautiful.

Us In A Photo Frame

The first day back at school felt like walking into a dream that had paused mid-sentence. The cold January air still lingered in the corridors, blazers buttoned up completely, hands shoved deep into pockets. Everyone was catching up—new year resolutions that wouldn't last, last-night memes, even the latest school gossip.
But I wasn't here for any of that. Not really.

I had one thing circling my mind, looping louder than the morning bell—Aaradhya's birthday. 31st wasn't too far. And I didn't want to mess this up. Not with something generic. Not with something guessed. I wanted something *hers*.

But how do you ask someone directly, 'What kind of gifts do you like?' without sounding like you're about to give one? So I took the long route—watching, listening, collecting clues like puzzle pieces. But even though I noticed her smallest details—how she braided her hair, how she tilted her head while reading, the way her eyes lingered on soft colors—I couldn't find anything giftable. Nothing felt right.

Midway through the month, I sat by the window seat in class, watching a sunless January afternoon dull everything outside, disappointed and blank. Judging by my face, Vansh leaned in and asked about me and I told him everything. He laughed and repeated what he'd said before.
But then, like always, he sighed, softened, and said, 'Okay, let me see what I can do.'
That's who he was—my fixer. No matter how scattered I was, he knew how to pull the pieces together. This time, his plan was simple but smart: he'd ask Aarohi to casually dig in. Not directly, but in a way that would feel natural—'What would make you happiest if he gifted you something?'
Clever. I agreed. I trusted him. I let it happen.
But I thought it'd be quick. But It wasn't.
On January 19th, I finally asked him if he'd found anything. He hesitated. I pressed, *'Usne bataya bhi ki nahi?'*
He replied quietly, *'Bataya to... par tere kaam ka nahi hai.'*
That sentence dropped like a stone. I begged, *'Bata na, yaar.'*
He avoided me, kept brushing it off. And when I pushed too hard, he finally said:
'Look... she didn't say anything useful. Just gift her something, anything. She'll like it. Trust me. I know what she told Aarohi—and you'll be happy to know it. But you'll be even happier if you hear it after her birthday.'

That only made it worse. I stopped bombarding him with questions, but my mind wouldn't stop spinning. And something else felt off. He wasn't irritated. Not really. He was... distant. I'd known him long enough to read between the silences. He shared everything with me—his pain, his random midnight thoughts. Why was he holding this back? Had I done something wrong? Why couldn't he just tell me? That day, I returned home—not empty-handed, but empty-hearted.

Two questions echoed in my mind on loop: What should I gift her? And why was Vansh behaving like this?

Since that day, Vansh had turned unusually quiet. He replied to my messages, sure—but only just. No extra words, no jokes, no late-night voice notes. Nothing that felt like him. I tried to figure out what was wrong, but he didn't explain.

When the final exam timetable was released, he stopped coming to school altogether.

So I called him but he didn't pick up. I figured Aarohi might know something, so I texted her. But her reply? *'Mujhe kya pata!'*

What kind of person says that? Didn't even know what was going on with her own partner. Or maybe she did and didn't want to share. Either way, it left me on my own.

'Maybe he's just busy studying,' I told myself. And I should be too.

February was close. But most unfortunately, exams were falling up all on Valentine's week. No plans, no confessions, no gestures—just pages to memorise and stress to juggle. And I still hadn't found a gift for her. Not for lack of trying. But nothing felt good enough.

I was stuck—between equations and emotions, revision and restlessness.

The last days of January brought rush with them. I still hadn't gotten her a gift, and her birthday was on the 31st. I kept up my desperate little research runs, overthinking—but eventually, I gave up. I didn't know what she'd like. But I also couldn't just show up empty-handed.

Then, on the 30th, an idea hit me. It wasn't brilliant—but it was something.

That night, once everyone had fallen asleep, I set up my little workspace. I pulled out a photo of hers—from *Chhath Pooja*—and started a glass painting.

I began with her face. It went well... until I reached the eyes. That part was way harder than I thought. I tried, gave up, and left them undrawn. Weird, maybe—but I had a fix in mind.

To fill the space, I added a simple 'Happy Birthday' in clean, block letters. And behind it, I pasted a collage of her photos—ones I'd saved in my books, used as bookmarks, tucked away for reasons I never admitted aloud. When I stepped back, it looked... perfect. At least to me.

I wrapped it in newspaper to keep it safe, then again with gift wrap.

Luckily, no one noticed anything.

I tucked it carefully into my school bag. And finally, I went to sleep. The next morning was waiting. So was she.

The sun hadn't even risen when I got ready and left. The bus arrived, and as I stepped in—there she was. walked to my seat, trying to calm my nerves. Then, mustering a little courage, I leaned forward and said, 'Happy Birthday, Aaradhya.' She smiled softly and replied, 'Thank you.' That should've been it. But my mind immediately jumped to the gift. I froze.

I wasn't ready. I didn't know how to give it.

I clutched my bag tighter. In that crowded bus, my courage gave out completely.

Even Vansh hadn't come to school. Who was going to help me then?

In my imagination, I handed her the gift with ease—like some hero in a scene.

But in reality, I was just... stuck, scared, silent. *There was another problem too*—our relationship wasn't public. We weren't out loud. And I couldn't just give her something in front of everyone.

That's when a plan hit me. During the third period, I took a backbench seat—last row. I quietly placed the wrapped gift inside the desk, like a secret mission. Then came lunch. As soon as the crowd rushed out, I ran to Aarohi.

'Please,' I begged, 'can you give this to her?' She looked at me like I was ridiculous.

'Tera gift hai, tujhe dena chahiye,' she denied.

'I know, yaar. But I don't have that courage. Please,' I urged. After some convincing—and a lot of pleading—she finally agreed.

I gave her one more instruction: 'Tell Aaradhya not to open it in school or in the bus. Say a girl gave it to her if anyone asks.' Aarohi nodded, and walked off with the gift.

I exhaled. Finally. But peace didn't last long.

In the bus, Aaradhya had her gifts out, showing off. Everyone was passing them around.

And there it was—mine. Still wrapped. Ashwin squinted at it, *'Yeh ab tak khula kyun nahi? Kisne diya?'* She replied, *'Shreya ne.'*

My stomach flipped. At least she didn't take my name. She wasn't opening it. Good. But then Ashwin pushed, 'Open it, yaar!'

'Ashwin ki toh—Please don't do it,' I screamed silently. But she gave in. Started peeling the gift wrap.

The newspaper layer was visible. Ashwin immediately blurted, *'Abe kya? Newspaper mein gift di hai?'*

It hit like a slap. Without thinking, I snapped, *'Arey, andar ka toh dekh le!'* And then I shut up, horrified. Ashwin looked at me, eyebrows raised.

As she finally uncovered the glass painting, Ashwin laughed again,

'*Dekh, bina aankhon wali chudail banayi hai!*' My face
burned.
Aaradhya stayed quiet. Not a word. Maybe she didn't like it.
But then, she finally said, '*Accha toh lag raha hai.*'
A small part of me relaxed. Maybe... she actually did?
I leaned back in my seat, heart thudding.

'*Chalo... aakhir ye bala to tali,*' I thought. I wasn't forcing
anything. But damn—it was hard. Really hard. Still, in the
end... maybe it all went right.

No sooner had I reached home than I rushed to Instagram,
straight to Aaradhya's chat. I couldn't hold back—I asked if
she liked the gift. The curiosity was eating me alive. I even
dropped an excuse before she replied: 'I didn't know your
choice... so this is what I managed.'
I kept hovering over the phone, refreshing, reopening the
chat. Half an hour later, her reply came.
'Seriously, how can someone gift something like this?'
My heart dropped. But before I could spiral, the next
message popped up.
'I was amused. I never thought someone would gift me
something like this. Thank you.'
Everything shifted. That single message turned all my worry
into something warm—into a kind of joy that didn't need
words.
I typed, '*Thank you ki kya zarurat hai..*'

Still, a small panic surfaced. I asked, *'Ghar pe to nahi bataya na?'*
She replied, *'Nahi... par ghar mein tumhara gift sabko bahut pasand aaya. Hum usse frame kar rahe hai.'*
'Wow,' I typed back. It felt surreal. Was it really that good? But then I wrote, 'It's just a small gift... nothing in front of what you gave me on my birthday.'
The chat drifted after that—into a soft reel of memories, little callbacks to the day, everything suddenly wrapped in a calm, happy haze.

Is It Really February?

February had entered the chat—but all it did was talk rubbish. I mean, how can February be like this? The best thing about it—Valentine's Week—was completely destroyed. Who decided exams should fall on these dates? I was forcing myself to study, and yeah, I did. But whether I remember a single thing is still a mystery.

Honestly, I was going to school just to see Aaradhya's face. But to my surprise, Vansh was back.

'Kaha the itne dino se?' I asked.

He smiled awkwardly. 'At home only.'

'Why didn't you respond to our calls and messages?'

'Vo... phone se door ho gaya tha kuch dino ke liye...'

I narrowed my eyes. *'Bhai se jhoot bolega? Sach sach bata kya hua tha?'*

After a pause, he finally muttered, *'Bas ek chhota sa jhagda hua tha...'*

Oh. That made sense now. No wonder Aarohi had acted so cold that day. So this was the reason behind his disappearance.

'Crybaby,' I thought to myself, half-annoyed, half-relieved. *'Hua kya tha?'* I asked.
But the way his face dropped—I let it go. Changed the topic. *'Accha vo chhod. Ye bata, ghoomne jaane ka plan kab banega?'* We'd been planning a boys' day out for a while.
'Ab to 12th mein hoga,' he said.
I laughed. *'Par tu pass hoga tab na!'*
The jokes picked up, and February started passing like the screen time of a Gen Alpha addict—rising by the hour.
Exams began on 6th Feb. Valentine's week wasn't a complete disaster, but it wasn't memorable either.
Still, it was Rose Day when I started learning more about her—her choices, her quirks. Like when I texted, 'If these exams weren't here, I'd have given you not just a rose... but a whole bouquet.'
And she replied, 'And I wouldn't have accepted it.'
When I asked why, she said, 'Because I'm loyal to sunflowers.'
That was it. I didn't argue. I was learning, right?
Teddy Day and Chocolate Day? I skipped mentioning them. No point—one wrong word and we'd end up arguing.
Hug Day was okay though. I wouldn't have minded being held by her warm arms. But Kisses? That was too far—not our thing, not now. Hugs were enough. But even that didn't happen.
Because of these stupid exams.
Funny thing? In the rush of revision and routines, we somehow managed to acknowledge most of the silly

days—but we forgot the only one that mattered—Valentine's Day, missed. Like a page we accidentally skipped while flipping too fast.
We barely got time to talk afterwards, and just like that, February passed—under the shadow of exams and days we couldn't hold onto.

March marched in with days marking a fresh beginning. 'I'm a 12th grader now...' I thought, sitting up in bed the morning after our final exam—Computer Science. The weight of the syllabus was off my chest, but something else felt light too. Free.

The school was closed, but our fun wasn't. That evening, Vansh and Rehan showed up at my place to drag me into a spontaneous badminton match. When we reached the court, Ashwin joined us too.
It wasn't empty. A couple was already there—playing in sync, fast, almost cinematic. Both of them looked fit, like they'd walked straight out of a sports ad. After a few minutes, they wrapped up and smiled politely as they left the court for us.
'Kash main bhi...' I mumbled.
Vansh laughed. 'This is called daydreaming.'

We got started. Rehan was on my side, and Vansh on the other. Ashwin, well... he was mostly missing the shuttle.

But I wasn't bad. Neither was Rehan. We made a solid team—and we won. As we high-fived, I couldn't help smiling. It wasn't about the game. It was about feeling alive again.

Eventually, everyone headed home. It was just me and Vansh walking back to his place. I sighed, almost to myself, 'I really want to play badminton with her.' No response.

I said it again, louder this time, hoping he'd catch on. Maybe offer a plan. A setup. Something.

But he didn't. Just a half-hearted reply: 'Let's chat later, I've gotta go somewhere.' And he left.

For a second, it stung. This wasn't like him. He usually fixed things, especially mine.

But maybe I was expecting too much. He had his own personal life too, and I can't just depend on him... I needed to learn to figure out my things myself.

By March 9, our results were out. Aaradhya came with her parents. I was there with mine too. Both of us had done better than before—like we were slowly learning how to balance love and academics without dropping either.
It didn't feel like victory. It felt like progress.

It was 11 March—the school reopening. While the principal gave the usual boring opening speech. we whispered through the assembly, playfully misinterpreting her words.

When We Explored Offline

We were there—in grade 12. I couldn't believe it. It was meant to happen, but still, it felt like we had won a championship. Only this time, the game ahead was going to be tougher. Most importantly—my accelerating obsession with Aaradhya.

In class, I'd just stare at her, making sure no one noticed. I'd pretend I was part of the group conversation, but my mind would drift—always to her, even during lectures.

Teachers weren't really teaching anything anyway—just walking in, announcing the syllabus, and leaving.

March wasn't harsh when it came to studies, but for my heart, it was intense. *We'd talk late into the night, even dream about each other... but reality was unforgiving.*

We had nothing in person. No romance. Not enough togetherness. Life was moving so bleak and slowly.

That's when I started planning—those coming days—I had to make them count. Because we were in 12th now.

And we didn't know how far the next year would take us from each other. The fear was eating me alive.

But I had to try. I had to make it worth something.

On a mid-April night, under a full moon, I was roaming around in the dark. There was a power cut—no light, no noise, just silence and shadows.

As I walked past the park, I saw couples—hands resting on shoulders, strolling together, exchanging soft laughter under the moonlight.

If only I had the courage to do that.

Life suddenly felt like something was missing.

Our growth—mine and Aaradhya's—was slow compared to those who had come together after us.

Vansh and Aarohi were already steps ahead—meeting often, even having dinners together.

How can people be so open? I bit my tongue, frustration boiling quietly inside me. I talked to Aaradhya about it—that I wanted us to be more active together, offline too. Maybe she wasn't ready either. But still... she agreed.

I had taken permission. That was the easy part.

But I didn't know how to do it—not with the weight of secrecy we had to carry. We needed privacy, and that made everything feel heavier than it should have been.

It was our first date—or maybe just a meet. The word *date* always felt a bit too serious for us, like something meant for people who had mastered romance already. We were just beginning to understand it.

Late April had just settled in, and I was nervous in a way I hadn't felt before. It wasn't like exam stress or stage fear—this was different, a pressure that came from wanting to be seen, really seen, by someone I cared for. I didn't know how these things worked, so I turned to Vansh, hoping he'd give me some kind of code. He just laughed and said, *'There's no secret, just do it.'*

So I did. I dressed up like it was some kind of festival, fixing imaginary creases and checking the mirror ten times. On my way, while waiting at a traffic light, I passed a flower shop and remembered her saying once—I'm loyal to sunflowers. I stopped, parked, and asked the vendor, *'Kitne ka hai ek?'* He said, '130 rupees.' They were fresh, shining in the evening light. I took three. It felt right.

When I reached the café, I thought I might be late, but she wasn't there. A few minutes later, she called—'Where are you? Why didn't you come?' That's when I realised she was nearby, just at the wrong place. I guided her, and soon, there she was. Her trench coat swayed slightly with the wind, her hair a little messy, her eyes searching—until they met mine.

We stepped in. The café smelled warm and welcoming. She smiled as she glanced through the menu, and I took the moment to hand her the bouquet. Her face lit up with surprise and delight. 'Wow!' she said, holding the flowers close, smiling like a child who had just been given their favourite candy. 'Thank you.'

That small thank-you untangled something in me. The awkwardness faded. She took pictures with the sunflowers, and I clicked them, *playing the role of her personal photographer* without complaint. We ate a light meal, spoke little, but the silence didn't feel heavy—it felt like comfort.

At one point, I asked, *'Ghar par kya bol ke aayi?'* She looked calm as she replied, 'That I'm out with friends. It's common. No one will suspect, don't worry.' And I didn't. For once, everything had aligned.

Later that night, she posted a private story—just a picture of the flowers on her lap. I smiled and posted one too. No captions. No tags. Just our little secret. The next day, she even changed her profile picture—her with the sunflowers, grinning. That was more than enough.

It wasn't perfect. It wasn't grand.
But it was ours. And that was all it needed to be. Because from from that day, something changed between us—we had grown closer. Not just in texts or calls, but in the real world too. It felt warmer, more real.

Soon after, summer vacation began. With it came a flood of project files and model assignments. At first, I told myself I'd finish everything early and then enjoy the rest of the days. But deep down, I knew—we were in 12th now. It wasn't the time to relax, not completely. Boards were no longer a distant threat; they were the horizon we were speeding toward.

Still, that didn't mean I had to live like a robot, studying 24/7. I found my own balance—work and fun, both. The weather helped. The trees outside were painted in fresh greens, some blooming into gentle hues. It wasn't perfect, not really. But it was beautiful in its own way, and perfect enough to make memories with her.

I had started planning, little by little—everything I ever wanted to do with her. And at the top of the list was the one thing I had once wished Vansh would help me with: a badminton date.

When I told Vansh about it, that Aaradhya and I were finally going to do it, he raised an eyebrow and said, 'Why don't we make it a double date? All four of us.'
'Accha idea hai, aajao,' I replied without hesitation.
He blinked, surprised. 'Really? Don't you want to spend personal time with her?'
I smiled. 'Yeah, I do. But maybe... all four of us will be better. Growing and bonding together.'

But when the day actually came, things didn't go exactly
how I had imagined. I was the first to arrive—maybe too
excited, maybe too nervous. Vansh and Aarohi showed up
next.
'Abhi tak aayi nahi?' Vansh asked, noticing my empty side.
I shook my head.
Aarohi chuckled, *'Uski to aadat hai late hone ki.* Even when
we girls meet, she's always the last to come.'
I nodded slowly. But last time... last time she wasn't late. On
our date.
And then she came—dressed in athletic wear like she'd
trained for this all her life. My breath caught a little.
We made teams—Vansh and I on one side, the girls on the
other. But clearly, we were outmatched. They crushed us. So
we switched. Now, I was paired with Aarohi, and Vansh
with Aaradhya. It felt weird. Too weird.
I couldn't play properly. I kept awkwardly distancing myself
from Aarohi, afraid to move too close. What if Vansh
misread something? What if Aaradhya thought I was being
inappropriate? The hesitation ruined my game, I did regret
it because they didn't even hesitate and beat us again.
Obviously. They had both the strong players on one side.

Vansh must've seen it in my face—my awkwardness, my
longing. 'Okay,' he said, grinning, 'let's swap teams again.
Aarohi and me, and Anuj and Aaradhya.'
'What?' I almost blurted, but it was happening. She was on
my team.

I tried to focus. But with her beside me, that close, I couldn't. What if I hit her with the shuttle? What if I made a fool of myself again?

But she played flawlessly. Each time I missed, she picked up. She carried the entire game on her back, and I just... watched. Mesmerised.
Even in that sporty outfit, she looked beautiful—maybe too beautiful for my comfort. But we won. Technically, I won. Because of her.

It wasn't the private date I had originally pictured, but it still felt special. The skies outside had turned grey; the wind was picking up. Aarohi had to leave before the rain hit, so Vansh and she left. And just like that, it was the two of us. Alone. She didn't look like she was in a hurry. I hesitated, then said, 'If you want to go, you can... Or we could play another match. As you wish.'
She smiled faintly. 'No more playing yaar, I'm tired. I'm just waiting. I called my sister, she's on her way to pick me up.'
Perfect. I had an excuse to stay—*'Ladki ko aise akele kaise chhod dun.'* Though something heavy stirred inside me. I wanted to be there for her. Not just today. Always.

The silence crept in, and to break it, I whispered, 'Thank you.'
'For what?' she asked.

'We couldn't have won if you hadn't carried us. You basically saved the game.'

She laughed. *'Nahi yaar, tumne bhi to accha khela.'*

'Me? Nah. *Mujhe to khelna bhi nahi aata.'*

And then, without thinking, I said what I had only rehearsed in my head so many times. *'Dekha nahi, tumhe dekhte dekhte maine kitni baar miss kiya.'* It slipped out. And it burned. But it was real. She blushed. Actually blushed.

Rain began to drum on the tin roof of the stadium, soft at first, then louder, like the soundtrack of something quietly beautiful.

She looked at me, half teasing, half wondering. *'Kab tak dekhta rahega mujhe aise? Humesha hi to dekhta hai. Bore nahi hota?'*

And I said, almost in a breath, *'Nahi hota, aur kabhi honga bhi nhi.'*

She leaned in. Just slightly. A little too close. My heart started pacing faster. Something grand was about to happen—I could feel it. Like time had paused for us.

And then her phone rang. She flinched back and picked it up. My heart dropped, crashing into the floor of reality. Again. I stared at the badminton court, still littered with a few feathers from the shuttlecock, and whispered inside, **Why does the best moment always have to come with an interruption?**

But maybe... maybe next time, it won't.

Is It Really That Hard?

It was her sister on the call. She said their father had come in
the car to pick her up. Before leaving, Aaradhya looked at me
and softly instructed, 'Don't follow me outside, okay?'
Neither did I have the courage to do so.

A few minutes later, when I finally stepped out, she was
gone. The road was empty, the rain still pouring, and I was
left standing there, alone. I picked up our rackets and closed
the gate behind me—not entirely, just slightly, as if some
part of me still waited for her to return. The rain refused to
stop.
As I stood under the tin roof, watching the drizzle blur
everything in front of me, one question kept echoing in my
head—What would've happened if her phone hadn't rung?
I didn't know, but I wanted to.
When the rain slowed to a drizzle, I ran toward home with
the racket cover over my head like a shield. Still, by the time I
reached, I was drenched—my clothes soaked by the rain, and
my mind soaked in that one unanswered moment.

We met many times after that—random, innocent, scattered across the early summer days. I studied too, sometimes. But that question stayed.

By the end of May, one evening, I was at Vansh's house. His parents had gone out of station, and he had called me over to keep him company. We were sitting on the terrace swing when, to my surprise, a scooty stopped near the gate.

Aaradhya. 'Why is she here?' I asked, eyebrows raised.

Vansh smirked. 'I called her. Aarohi's coming too.' I blinked. 'She agreed?'

'Only because I told her you'd be here,' he said, giving me a knowing look.

I stood there speechless. I couldn't wrap my head around it—how did she manage the time? What excuse did she make at home? It was like we were getting bolder... maybe even a little *besharam*. And honestly, it made me nervous.

She smiled when she saw me and followed us upstairs to the terrace. The breeze was warm, the sky dimming gently. She sat on the swing. I remained standing, unsure, until she said, 'Baith na.'

I sat. Close. Too close. The gap between us, barely a few centimeters. My body stiffened, my hands unsure what to do. I looked at the sky, trying to act normal, but my cheeks betrayed me—I was definitely blushing.

She broke the silence with a sudden question, 'Homework complete *hua*?'

Homework? Damn—I had completely forgotten about the project files.

'*Nahi, main toh bhool hi gaya tha ki project bhi hai,*' I confessed. I asked about her, she giggled and said, '*kab ka ho gaya mera.*'

She was scrolling through her phone when it suddenly slipped from her hand. In panic, she lunged to catch it—her hand met mine, and in that one second, our fingers clasped. Her touch—warm, soft, feather-light—felt electric.
She caught her phone and exhaled in relief. 'Thank you, *bach gaye.*'

But I wasn't listening to the words. My mind was too busy engraving that one touch. My heartbeat had gone completely off rhythm.
Vansh returned a few minutes later, snacks in one hand, a deck of cards in the other. Aarohi came with him. We played cards under the moonlight, laughing and bluffing, the night folding into something light and fleeting.
At my insistence, Vansh even ordered Coke from Blinkit.
When it arrived, Aarohi grimaced and said, '*Chi re, kaisa ladka hai tu. You don't even drink?*'
'Drink?' I frowned. '*Kabhi socha bhi nahi. Mujhe nahi pasand.*'

I hated it, actually. The way it changed people—louder, messier, crueler. That part of the night left a sour taste. My mood dipped a little.
But I kept replaying one thing in my head—not the game, not the argument, not even the Coke.
Just her hand in mine. That one accidental moment I didn't want to let go of.

A few days later, we were at Nani's place in Bhilai. All my aunts had gathered there with their kids—my cousins. The house felt alive, chaotic, the kind of noise that's comforting because it means you belong.

Among them was my elder cousin sister—the same one who, during our last visit, had said I was the kind of guy no girl would ever like. It had stuck with me, that statement. Quietly. It hurt. So this time, I was excited to prove her wrong.
I told her everything. From the first day to all the memories we'd shared over the past few weeks.
She just laughed. *'Kya mazak karta hai re tu! Kaunsi movie dekh ke aaya hai?'*
I didn't blame her. I knew how all of it sounded—unreal. Especially the birthday part. Even I sometimes thought, how could something so filmy happen to someone like me? But it did happen. And I was proud. Lucky. Maybe even special.

So I tried to convince her. I pulled out my phone and
showed her our Snapchat chat from my birthday. Still, she
didn't budge.

*'Tu ne khud ka fake account bana liya hoga. Kya proof hai ki
woh ladki asli hai?'*

That hit me. What? Why would I fake all that? For what?
I stomped away in frustration, then came back, determined
to shut her up for good. I opened my private album—the
one with photos of me and Aaradhya. Her expression
shifted.

'Really?' she whispered, staring at the screen.
I couldn't tell if it was disbelief or envy. But I just stood
there, confused. Why was it so hard to believe someone like
me could be liked back?

Few days later, we returned home. School had already
reopened—we were late. I'd missed the first day.
It had been a while since I saw Aaradhya in person. Sure,
we'd been texting and calling, but the offline vibe—the way
her presence made things feel real—was missing. I wanted to
see her. Just see her.
On my second day back, the teachers asked for our projects.
I had completely forgotten. Caught up in the rush of Bhilai,
cousins, stories, and memories, I'd ignored homework. And
the first-term exams were around the corner.

I rushed through assignments and took a couple of days off to finish everything. Aaradhya wasn't coming to school either. I found out she had a fever.

I texted her immediately, asking if I could visit—just to make sure she was fine.

She replied, 'No need. *Papa-mummy* are here. I'll be okay. It's not serious.'

But I was still worried. Possessiveness? Maybe. Care? Definitely. I just told her, 'Promise me you'll tell me the moment you feel okay. We'll meet, *pakka?*'

She replied with a smiley. That was it. I wasn't sure if that was a yes or just her way of ending the topic.

But something changed after that. Subtly. Silently. And two weeks before the exams, I felt it. Maybe... *maybe she didn't like how much I cared. Like I crossed a line I couldn't see.*

If Only Painkillers Could Kill My Pain

It was one of those rare school mornings when the bus felt emptier than usual—Ashwin hadn't come, and even Aarohi was absent. Just the two of us in our usual seats, but the silence was heavier than ever.

She didn't look at me immediately. Just kept her eyes on the window, earphones plugged in but not playing anything. I could tell—she was thinking. Something she had rehearsed. After a while, she pulled one earphone out and turned slightly toward me. 'I wanted to say something,' she began. That sentence alone made my heart skip.
'We need to study seriously now,' she said. 'Boards are closer than they feel. And honestly, *hum thoda zyada hi... involved ho gaye hain.*'
I didn't know how to respond. My silence stretched between us like a thread I was scared to snap.
'*Matlab,*' she continued, 'it's not like I don't enjoy it—ye sab, time with you, the memories. But thoda risky ho gaya

hai. What if someone sees us? *Har baar jhooth bolna padta hai ghar pe. Dar-dar ke jeena pasand hai kya?'*

That last line hit me hardest. I'd never thought of it that way—from her side. The lies, the tension, the fear of being caught… for me, it had been exciting. For her, maybe a ticking clock. 'So…' I asked, voice low. *'Ab?'*
She exhaled, slowly. *'Bas. Ab se offline thoda pause. School aur bus tak theek hai. Baaki sab online. Jaise pehle tha.'*
The way she said it made it sound so… temporary. So logical. But my heart didn't care for logic. It cared for her.
I said, *'Theek hai.'* What else could I say?
We both looked forward again, not saying another word. The bus turned a corner. A street full of yellowed trees passed by. Just yesterday I'd imagined walking those roads with her again. Today, we were already taking steps back. We hadn't broken up. Nothing was over. And yet, something had changed.

The pause was meant for the exams. And I meant to respect it. I gave it my all—studied harder than ever, stayed home, kept chats limited to short goodnights or occasional online updates. She gradually messaged less. School days became a blur of bus rides and quick greetings, her time occupied with friends, mine buried in books.
During exams, even that faded. On the way there, we revised silently. On the way back, we debated MCQs and answers. No room left for love. No time for longing.

But it wasn't in vain—we had done our best. We made the pause worth the cost.
And then... exams ended.

I remember the moment I saw her again properly, really saw her after the last paper. I rushed to her like I'd waited months just to say one thing: *'Ab to pause khol le na?'*

But she blinked and replied, calm as ever,
'Aise hi nahi reh sakte? Aise accha lagta hai... I mean, vaise bhi lagta tha, but at least we weren't lying to our parents or living in fear.'
And just like that—everything inside me collapsed.
I stood still. Numb. Processing her words like they were another exam question I couldn't crack. Was that it? Were we... done? After everything we had been to, how could she say that?
Before I could even respond, Aarohi pulled her away.
I couldn't breathe. I couldn't think. My throat felt tight, heart heavy. I walked home like I was dragging grief on my back. The moment I reached, I opened my phone and texted her: 'Why did you say that? How could you?'
I didn't expect her to reply. But she did, in the evening.
'What did I do?' Followed by two laughing emojis.
'I'm about to cry and you're laughing?' I replied.
'Aree rona mat, pagal,' she typed back. 'I meant I'm not going anywhere. I just meant we should stick to the limit we set.'

I was half-relieved. But not fully. Why couldn't we just be…
everything again?

I told her. I sent crying emojis, poured my pain into the
screen.
She replied, 'Oh ho! I mean, not totally. But we were
meeting too frequently. Let's just make it more… occasional.
We have to study too, right?'
I felt lighter. But also hollow. As if I'd won something but
lost the joy in it. She said it so casually—like she was tired of
it all. Tired of me. I cried that night. The Fear She had, it
crept inside me and became mine, did she forget it?

In Dependence On Pause

The results were way better this time. The pause had worked. She had scored 89%. I was proud—so proud. I did well too... close enough. But my marks stayed a secret, hidden under the pile of emotions I hadn't yet sorted.

School reopened—but not like before.
It reopened under the weight of her 'limits.'
As if something beautiful had been folded into a plain friendship.As if we were just... platonic. Or worse—strangers who used to be something.
I told Vansh everything—how I felt like I was walking next to her but couldn't reach her anymore.
He stood by me like he always did, nodding through my breakdowns, offering silence where I needed it most, and words when I ran out of mine.
But I couldn't hold it in anymore. A few days later, I texted her. It was one of those restless nights. I had typed and deleted so many times, scared I'd sound too clingy again. But

I couldn't keep it in anymore. I finally sent her a long message:

'I don't know what's going on... You feel so different now. You barely reply, you sound cold, and even when you talk—it's like you're just being formal. You said we'll meet occasionally, I agreed. But now it feels like you're just... done with us. *Itna distance kyun?*'
I stared at the screen, heart pounding. A minute passed. Then five. I was about to shut the phone in frustration when the typing dots appeared.
'*Tu overthink kar raha hai...* I'm just trying to stay focused. We both are. You were the one who said we need to study seriously.'
'*Haan* but I didn't mean cutting off all feelings. I feel like you're slipping away... and I'm still stuck on the last time you smiled at me for real.'
She was silent for a while. I thought maybe I said too much. Then she replied—'Sorry... Maybe I was being too strict with myself. Mujhe laga tum bhi samjhoge... but I didn't realise itna hurt ho raha hai tujhe. It wasn't intentional.'
That reply hit something in me. I said: 'I know. But please don't act like we're strangers in school. Don't keep punishing me for caring too much.'
Her next message brought me some warmth back.
'Okay. Let's not go back to how it was exactly... but we'll be more natural, more us. Not too much, not too less. *Balance bana lete hain.* Happy?'

'*Thoda zyada bhi chalega*,' I replied, half-smiling.
'*Pagal*,' she typed with a smiling emoji.

And in that moment, my side was heard. A mutual understanding settled. *The string between us that was stretched to the point of snapping...* held.
She wasn't entirely back. Not like before. But she was warm again. Not cold. And that was enough—for now.

Days passed. It was mid-August. Independence Day. Patriotic songs echoed through the streets, loudspeakers buzzing from every corner of the neighborhood. Our school campus was decked out in orange, white, and green. As our class was assigned the anchoring duties, we were all in traditional-formals—kurta, badges, even those small Indian flags pinned to our chests. Everything felt alive... except me. Ever since that pause, I had felt like we were living in a duller version of the same life. Same faces, same places, but everything just... less. It wasn't that she stopped talking. But the way she talked? It had changed. Formal. Filtered. No spark. And honestly, I was scared to admit—I was missing her version that was just for me.
Vansh noticed, obviously. He always did.
On our way out, he gave me a nudge and smirked, '*Kyu? Tumhara to vo pause khatam ho gaya tha na? Baat kyu nahi kar rahe?*'
I didn't reply. Just walked away. Some wounds aren't meant for friends to treat.

That day, because of low attendance, some buses were merged. Vansh ended up in my bus. He sat with Aarohi, and the two of them were as usual—teasing, laughing, whispering secrets. I didn't even try to sit beside Aaradhya. She was far ahead, and more importantly—Ashwin was there. If he found out anything between us, he'd turn it into the next gossip session for the entire school.
But when Vansh's stop came closer, he did what Vansh does best—interfere in the best and worst ways possible.
'Jaa na yaar. Baat kar. Itni chup kyun hai vo?'
He literally pushed me to get up and sit beside her. And I did.
For a second, it felt like the world had paused—not the kind we forced on ourselves, but the kind where only one person matters. She looked at me, surprised... but soft. That softness I missed.

Vansh, of course, took a photo before getting off. We both saw him do it. No words—just a smirk and a camera click. That photo? I saved it. A memory I didn't know I'd need.
As the bus moved again, I asked her why she'd been so silent. She just smiled and said, 'Aarohi was busy... I didn't want to disturb them, that's all.' Simple. No drama. No overthinking.
And after Vansh left, she was really back—laughing softly, shoulders relaxed, eyes meeting mine like they used to.
I thought maybe... maybe we were healing.

But I didn't know what was coming.
Because someone else was about to enter my life.
And if only—If only she had never come...

A Stranger Crossing A Line

On a breezy September morning, the girls in our class were casually gossiping with our class teacher when she mentioned that a new girl from Xavier's Jaipur branch would soon be joining us. Later that day, Aaradhya texted me the same story. It was just after our second term exams when that unfamiliar face finally walked into class—wearing the Jaipur variant of our school's uniform. She looked stunning, no doubt, but in front of Aaradhya, she was like a sheep trying to stand against a lioness. With her round-frame spectacles and easy smile, she blended in with the other girls far too quickly.

Since I had nothing to do with her, I didn't even know her name for days—until the day our class was in charge of the school assembly. I hadn't been given any role, so I stood in the usual line, but the new girl had been assigned one. Aaradhya was the compere that day. When she called out the name for the pledge, that's when I heard it for the first time—'Shivani'. Most unfortunately, she turned out to be a total duffer. She didn't even recite the pledge properly. Like, seriously? How can someone forget something they've been hearing daily since childhood?

After the assembly, I said to Aaradhya: *'Ye kis gadhi ladki ko pledge de diya tha?'*
She didn't defend her, but she didn't side with me either. All she said was, *'Chhod na.'*
They had become friends. And we... We were something more than that. Maybe that's why *she couldn't see what that friendship might cost her.*

Aaradhya and Shivani were sitting together that day. Even though Shivani was a commerce student, we had a few common subjects, so we shared some classes. It was English period, and maybe Aaradhya had told her what I said after the assembly, because I caught Shivani staring at me from the next row. I was already looking at Aaradhya, and Shivani's eyes accidentally met mine. I quickly looked down at my open notebook and started pretending to write something.
But just when I thought she had looked away, a paper ball hit the back of my head.
I stood up, annoyed. *'Ye kya hai?'* She pointed at the paper ball and said, *'Khol to.'*
Inside, there was a Snapchat username. *'Snapchat hai, add kar lena,'* Shivani said. What even was that way of asking? So random.

Aaradhya didn't say anything. She knew where my loyalty
lay. Maybe that's why she let it go. But I didn't add Shivani.
Even when she sent me a request later, I left it pending.
Until she texted me on WhatsApp: *'Accept kar na.'*
That's when I finally accepted. She messaged right away:
'Please don't reply on WhatsApp, *mummy dekh leti hai*. I
don't have a personal phone yet.'
She felt like a girl straight out of the early 2000s—no
personal phone, strict parents. I said okay, and then she
switched topics, asking me about the school.
I replied, 'Firstly, I'm not a commerce student, so I've got no
clue. Secondly, what's the point of talking about it now?
Even if the teachers suck, you can't change much. Just
cooperate, we'll be done with school soon. But if you're not
happy, you can always repeat 11th in another school.'
She didn't know what to say. Instead, she said, *'Hindi mein
bolna.'*
I didn't bother replying. Then she added, *'Mujhe aane ka
mann to nahi tha, but papa ka urgent transfer ho gaya.
Government flat bhi chala gaya,* so had to come with them.'
So that was her story—simple. But it didn't stay simple for
long. Especially once her ambitions started showing.

The first sign came when she started calling me every night.
Not for studies. Just random *bakwaas* about me, about
herself, about everything. She would ask the weirdest
personal questions—*'Kya pasand hai khane mein?* Favourite

colour? Favourite subject? Book? Music? Family? Crushes?'
Like she was collecting biodata.
I kept it plain. 'I don't have any crushes.'
I wasn't about to spill my secrets to someone I barely knew.
She even started sending snaps—different outfits, different
poses—like she wanted me to comment on them. I didn't. I
left her on seen.
Then she switched tactics—started video calling me. At first,
I let them ring out. But when she began spamming, I gave
up and picked one.
She'd be on the other side, all chirpy, *giving me a house tour
happily like we were long-lost friends. 'Yeh mera room, yeh
mera chhota bhai, yeh meri drawings...'* Then she'd ask,
'Accha hai na?'
I'd just nod and say, *'Haan, accha hai.'* Even if it wasn't.

Her calls, her questions, her endless chatter—it was
becoming too much. There's a fine line between curiosity
and intrusion, and she was slowly crossing it. I wasn't
entertained anymore. I was exhausted.
That night, I finally told Aaradhya.
She paused after hearing everything. 'She really did all that?'
There was disbelief in her voice, the kind that hurts when
someone you trusted doesn't live up to it.

I nodded. She sighed, then said, 'Just tell her you're busy. Say
you're preparing for pre-boards. That's the easiest way to

keep your distance without sounding rude.' It was the perfect excuse. I used it.

The calls stopped. But the texts? Still coming. Still constant. I had already told Vansh about everything. He gave me that look—the one where he knew I wasn't being fully honest with myself.

'Do whatever you like,' he said casually. 'Just don't let her become a home wrecker.'

I laughed awkwardly. 'It's not like that, man. It's just... she's too much sometimes. I feel suffocated.'

'Then just say it. Be upfront. If she hasn't done anything wrong, you don't have to be cruel, but you don't have to suffer either. Your peace matters more.'

He was right. I knew he was right. But I couldn't say it. I didn't want to hurt her feelings. She hadn't done anything wrong. She was just... too involved. Too soon.

So, I let it be. Until she took things further. She started finding me—Offline, in school.

One day, she just kept talking—random things, nonsense really—and all I did was nod or mumble, 'hm', every now and then. I didn't add anything on my own. I didn't care to.

Vansh and Aaradhya had both told me—without saying much—just through a few exchanged glances and gestures: get rid of her somehow. And trust me, I had tried. But I couldn't—not without being harsh. And she hadn't really done anything wrong. That was the problem.

Most of the time, I tuned out. But sometimes, when she talked about books or novels, I'd actually listen. One day, out of nowhere, she said, 'I like romance,' with a tone that felt like a flirt. I shut it down immediately. 'I prefer thrillers, to be honest.'

She went quiet for a second. Maybe that was the first time I'd pushed back.

Still, as time passed, I found myself enjoying some of her chats. Shivani had slowly become someone I didn't mind texting. Maybe even liked texting. She wasn't unbearable anymore. Her topics had changed—shifted into the zone of what I liked. Now I knew why she'd asked so many questions earlier—she was collecting data. Smart move.

But even in those moments, there was a dull ache inside me. I missed the old Aaradhya.

She had promised she'd come back to how she used to be. She said she would. But she didn't. And it hurt more than I let on. She had chosen studies, and maybe that was the right thing... maybe.

But still, I couldn't help but think—Were marks more important than me? Was I that easy to leave behind?

In that silence, in that ache, it was Shivani who stayed. She didn't know anything about me and Aaradhya, but she stayed anyway and *played an important role in reuniting us.*

A Drunk 18 Year Old Teen

A few days before my birthday, I told Aaradhya, 'It's been so long... I feel empty. We should meet.' I was practically begging her, trying to make her understand what I couldn't say out loud.

But she gave an excuse—*'Mere parents allow nahi karenge,'* she said.

'But I know you can convince them... please,' I typed, holding on to hope.

She replied, 'It's not possible. We'll meet later. *Vaise bhi school mein to milte hi hain na.'*

A strange weight settled on my chest. Heavy and suffocating. Why had she become like this? Did she find me annoying now? Did she not love me anymore?

A thousand questions flooded my mind, none with answers. The next day at school, I was unusually quiet, sitting with Vansh, trying to talk but drifting. My head fell to the desk, the cold surface grounding me for a second.

Vansh got up to leave, and that's when Shivani appeared beside me. I wasn't in the mood to deal with her—not today. I guess Vansh noticed, because he stepped in and casually pushed her back, as if to say, 'Not now.'

But Shivani didn't give up easily. She kept coming back, checking on me, her eyes full of concern. I didn't say a word. I wasn't angry at her. I was just... broken over Aaradhya. Later, when Vansh told me that Shivani had asked him about my behavior and he'd been blunt with her, I felt a twinge of guilt. She didn't deserve that.
So I messaged her that night: 'I'm sorry.'
She replied immediately, 'Why were you like that today?'
I didn't know what to say. I couldn't just tell her the truth. After a pause, I wrote: 'Exam stress.'
She sent back a whole paragraph, scolding me gently—reminding me to stay strong, to not take pressure. She cared. Genuinely.
And then, suddenly, she wrote: *Ek baat bolu?*
'Go ahead, type it,' I replied.
'Can we be best friends?'
I paused. With Aaradhya, I never had to think about that question. It just happened, naturally. But here, with Shivani—it was complicated. I didn't want to hurt someone who genuinely cared about me. But I also couldn't let her think there was more between us than there was. I would never cheat. Aaradhya still had my heart, even if she wasn't around like she used to be.
After thinking for a while, I typed: 'Okay.'

She sent a long string of happy emojis and messages. She was thrilled.

I didn't go to school for the next few days. There wasn't a real reason—I just didn't feel like going. Everything felt dull. Quiet. Empty.

During those days, I picked up a few new novels I'd bought, finally finishing some. While sorting through old books, I opened one of my romance novels—and a photo of Aaradhya slipped out. I had *kept her pictures as bookmarks* once, back when love felt alive.
I stared at it for a long time, my fingers brushing the edge like it could take me back.
Those days... they were something else.
Now? These days felt like nothing. No meetups. No late-night talks. No spark. Just silence. And with that silence, my birthday arrived.

It was my birthday, and like every other student obligated by custom and silent expectations, I brought chocolates to school. It had become a sort of algorithm—regular ones for classmates, Dark Chocolates for those who mattered, and an Oreo Silk, carefully tucked away for my 'Miss Drama Queen.'

The moment I stepped into class, a strange, involuntary smile tugged at my lips—one I wasn't even aware of until it settled. Maybe it was the sight of her. Aaradhya, sitting quietly in her spot, smiling faintly, almost like she had been waiting for this moment too.

I walked to my bench, trying to look casual, and was greeted by Ashwin and Aarohi in unison—'Happy Birthday, Anuj!'—their voices echoing louder than needed, yet welcome.
I thanked them with a nod, still glancing her way, hoping—expecting something from her.
And then she said it.
'Happy Birthday, Anuj,' her voice soft, like she didn't want the world to hear, just me.
The exact words she had written last year too.
Something about it felt achingly familiar, but this time the nostalgia wasn't warm. It was cold, distant—like remembering a home you can't return to.
I stared at her for a second, wondering if that was all—just a wish? No card, no gift, no small note she used to hide behind my books?
But then she leaned slightly closer and whispered, *'Gift to mil hi gaya hoga...'* and for a moment I froze.
When? What did she mean? Was she teasing, or was she serious?
'Hain?' I asked, already feeling my heartbeat quicken.
She smiled like she held a secret, then said, *'Instagram check kiya?'*

I shook my head, lips parting to ask more, but she turned away, casual as ever, as if she hadn't just tossed a mystery into my day. I tried to stay present, enjoy the wishes, the little surprises, but my mind remained tangled in her words. What could it be? A post? A collage? A message she couldn't say aloud?

Later, when it came time to distribute the chocolates, I walked up to her and handed over one bar, then three extra—hoping she'd read between the lines. She looked up, smiled again, and said, 'Happy Birthday' once more.

Then she extended her hand for a handshake.

I took it, hesitantly at first, but her palm was soft, grounding—and I held on. For a second too long. Maybe two.

She chuckled, and said, *'Chhodega bhi ab?'* with her eyebrows raised just enough to make me feel like a caught thief.

I let go immediately, my face hot with embarrassment, but a part of me didn't want to.

Then came Shivani. She stood up, holding a small wrapped box, smiling like she had waited all day for this.

'Happy Birthday, Anuj,' she said, her voice bright.

'Thank you,' I replied with a polite nod, accepting the gift.

Among the boys, only Ashwin gave me something—a cheap fountain pen—but I appreciated it. **Sometimes even small gestures say more than expensive ones.**

When the final bell rang and the noise of birthday chants faded, I handed a Dark Chocolate to Shivani, secretly we were best friends right?

I gave another to Vansh, my usual way of saying thanks without much drama. Predictably, he grinned and shouted, *'Isse kya hoga hume to party chahiye!'* and the boys around us erupted in excitement.

I laughed it off, dodged the idea, and slipped away before it gained traction.

On the bus ride home, Aaradhya and Ashwin wouldn't stop pestering me about Shivani's gift. Aaradhya especially kept glancing toward the box like it held a bomb instead of a birthday present.

Eventually, she said, 'Open it, na,' and because it came from her, I did.

I untied the orange ribbon slowly, peeled off the red wrapping paper, and revealed a small box—probably holding an accessory. I opened it. It was a watch.

But the dial wasn't ordinary—it had a tiny heart inside. Bright. Obvious. Loud. Too loud.

Ashwin burst out laughing, already coming up with lines to tease me. But I wasn't listening to him—I was looking at Aaradhya. Her expression had shifted—still, unreadable, but her silence was louder than the jokes around us. She didn't say a word, just turned to look out the window. But the tension in her jaw, the sudden stillness in her shoulders—it said everything.

As if she was thinking, Shivani is crossing a line.

Or maybe, Why didn't I do more?

I stared at the watch for a while. Its ticking felt heavier than it should.

Time—it was mocking me. Moving forward whether I was ready or not.

When I got home, I didn't waste a second hiding the watch. Something about it—about what it implied—made me feel uneasy. A gift like that didn't belong in plain sight.

Once I changed into my old, comforting home clothes, I picked up my phone, heart racing.

There was still something left—her gift. Aaradhya's. Something that might bring back a bit of the magic that had been slipping away, day by day.

When I unlocked my phone and opened Instagram, Aaradhya's name was right at the top—two messages waiting. My heart jumped a little.

The first one was simple—a thank you for the Oreo Silk I'd given her.

The second... was wrapped in the gift format. A digital ribbon over a box. I tapped it.

The ribbon untied. The lid lifted. And then came the message—long, heartfelt, impossible to scroll past quickly—

"Happy Birthday, Dear Anuj

From the first time I saw you after covid on 22 March, 2022 to what you are today—
A journey I'll ever cherish, keep close to my heart, and continue to love.

I will never forget the days we spent together, every small detail etched in memory.
Do you remember 19 January 2023, when I sent you an indirect message, hinting I had a crush on you?
On 23rd January, we were alone, rehearsing for the skit script.
And then, on my birthday, when you called me beautiful—you became my *pasandida* male from that moment on.
It was 16 February when you called me your best friend on Snapchat, and the way you cared from March to July made me feel so deeply loved.
By 16 July, I began to wonder if you might like me back—I started putting effort into myself, hoping you'd feel proud of me too.
And then 16 October, 2023… when we finally became a 'we'. It felt like a dream I never wanted to wake up from.
What followed felt like a movie. A heart-touching, imperfect, beautiful story.
29 October—we quarreled over chocolates but made up like little kids.
Diwali, November—you called me 'Miss Gorgeous' and made me feel like I was glowing inside.

25 March, 2025—our first real date. It started awkward, but you made it warm, so real. I still have those sunflowers you gave me—they're dried now, but I've kept them safe.
We kicked off our summer vacation with that double date with Vansh and Aarohi, and I remember you praising my skills.
Then there was May, when you touched my hand... and I felt like, in that small moment, our souls brushed too.
There's so much more—laughter, fights, apologies, secrets, dreams—moments that words fall short of capturing.
All I can say is that I love you. And I wish you all the happiness and success this world can offer.
May this birthday of yours be as wonderful as you are.
With all my love,
Your Aaradhya...
Once again, Happy Birthday."

I stared at the message, eyes fixed, heart slowly swelling with emotions I couldn't name properly.
How do you respond to something like that?
How do you thank someone for turning your memories into a timeline so poetic, so personal, that it felt like someone had poured love into every date, every word?
Aaradhya hadn't just written a message. She had gifted me a story. Our story. Folded into time. Every line was a timestamp etched in feeling.
I sat in silence for a long while. 'What else could mark the beginning of adulthood better than this?'

And as I held my phone, rereading the message again and
again, one thought lingered above all: I was still hers.
Even if the world shifted beneath my feet, I wanted this story
to keep going. I didn't know how to reply to that heartfelt
message—I really didn't. It brought with it not just
happiness, but something deeper. A flicker of *hope*.
Hope that maybe—just maybe—she was coming back to
her old self. That the distance I had felt for months was
finally dissolving, gift-wrapped in words. It felt like her real
present wasn't the message... but the possibility of us again.
The next day at school, I couldn't hide my happiness. I told
her how much it meant to me, how much she still meant to
me. She smiled. Just that.
Not the warmth I had expected. Not the softness from
before. A smile, small and quick, like a guest knocking at a
closed door, not sure if they're welcome.
And in that moment, I realised something painful.
She was slipping through my fingers. I was still holding
on—tightly, desperately—but she had already let go.
A line from Murakami's Norwegian Wood echoed in my
mind: ***"Our faces were no more than ten inches apart,
but she was light-years away from me."***
I had never felt something so distant, so close.

It was Shivani who stayed by my side during those days. My parents had left for Delhi to attend Mum's cousin sister's wedding—practically my aunt. They didn't take me along; pre boards were near, and they didn't want distractions. Instead, they asked the woman who lived next door to help with my lunch and dinner for four days.

I had tried convincing Aaradhya to visit. I even said I was alone. But she didn't come.

'Not now,' she said.

'Then when?' I had asked, hoping for something—anything.

'Just soon,' she replied, and left it at that.

I sighed. The gap between us felt more real with every unanswered question.

One afternoon, our neighbour wasn't home, so I had to manage on my own. I knew I could cook a little, but I didn't get the chance to. Shivani showed up, unannounced.

'Let's go out,' she said.

I hesitated but eventually put on a simple jacket. We were best friends now, and no one should have reason to comment—still, I made sure to keep my distance.

We went to a nearby panipuri stall, and then she surprised me by dragging me toward a billboard that read Belgian Waffle. I tried a waffle for the first time that day.

'Accha tha na?' she asked, smiling.

I nodded back with a faint smile.

Then she looked down at my wrist, at the watch she'd given me, and said, 'Let's take a pic.'

I didn't stop her, but I kept my distance in the frame.

'Don't post it anywhere. Not even in your private story,' I said.
'Why not?' she asked, raising a brow.
'Just don't,' I said softly.
She didn't ask more, but the suspicion in her eyes lingered. I just couldn't risk it. If Aaradhya saw, she might misunderstand—and I wasn't ready to lose her completely, not even in silence.
Shivani dropped me home, then opened the Activa's storage. A brown bottle peeked out.
'Beer?' I asked, narrowing my eyes.
'It's fruit beer. Not alcoholic. Chill!' she grinned.
'I don't drink,' I replied flatly.
'At least let me come inside,' she said, dramatically. I didn't want to be rude, so I let her in.
She opened the bottle, poured two glasses, and took a sip. Then she turned to me and said, 'Your turn.'
'I'm okay,' I muttered, unsure how to say no without upsetting her.
She laughed, stepped closer, glass in hand. A little too close. A strange chill ran down my spine as she tilted the glass toward my lips. I resisted—but not for long. The drink touched my tongue. It wasn't as bad as I had imagined.
I stood up and, without saying much, took the glass from her. Two sips. Three maybe. That was all I could take.

'Accha kiya na, main aa gayi?' she said with a proud smirk. I nodded, unsure whether it was gratitude or just politeness. She left after that.

My parents returned a week before Diwali. That year, Diwali and Halloween fell on the same day. My feed was full of reels with quirky captions like #Diwaloween.
But for me, none of it mattered. Not festivals, not lights, not reels.
All I could think about was this strange hollow—between Aaradhya's silence, Shivani's closeness, and the uncertain space in between.

A Change I Long For

Mum and Dad were caught in a cleaning frenzy—dusting, scrubbing, wiping corners like we lived in a round house with no end. Every time I paused, they dragged me back in. 'Why do we need to do this much?' I groaned more than once. But finally, after two or three days of relentless effort, the chaos settled.

On the morning before Diwali, I was sent to the market to buy *pooja samagri*. The streets were jammed—bustling with noise, chatter, and the clashing scents of incense, sweets, and sweat. I weaved through the crowd when suddenly, someone familiar appeared in the swirl of colours and motion. Aaradhya. She stood beside her father, visibly surprised to see me. Her eyes widened, and I couldn't help but smile—genuinely. For a second, I thought maybe we'd walk a bit together, maybe talk. But my smile faded as her father stepped into view.

She gave a small wave, smiling politely. I returned it and greeted him with a respectful *'Namaste.'* He seemed pleased and struck up a quick chat—asked what brought me here.

'I came to pick up stuff for the *pooja*,' I said.

He smiled and told me they were out shopping for clothes. Apparently, Aaradhya had been pestering him to buy her a new dress for Diwali. I chuckled.

'She didn't let us rest until we agreed,' he said.

Aaradhya looked away, clearly embarrassed. But just then, her eyes landed on my wrist—the watch. The one Shivani had given me.

Something shifted in her face. Her smile dimmed, her eyes dulled. It was a tiny moment, but unmistakable. She turned abruptly and said, *'Papa, chalo, chalte hain.'*

My mouth opened slightly—searching for something to say. I managed a soft 'Bye,' but she didn't respond. She just walked away, disappearing into the crowd with her father, her silence echoing louder than the honks and vendor calls around me.

I stood there, trying to make sense of it all. Was she... angry? At the watch? At me?

Had I done something wrong? Worn something I shouldn't have? But then again—didn't she do things too? Things that hurt me, confused me?

Still... her eyes—how they changed in that moment—they haunted me the rest of the walk home. I quickened my pace through the market, phone already in my hand, fingers

trembling as I messaged her right there and then: *'Are you fine? Gussa to nahi ho? Aise gusse mein papa ko le gayi?'*
Her reply didn't come immediately. Two hours passed. Each minute felt like a grain of salt being rubbed into my skin.

Then finally, just one message— *'Tumhe kya.'*
It stung. I stared at the screen, unsure if it meant anger, indifference, or heartbreak. But I shot back, heart pounding: 'Wdym *mujhe kya?* I care about you, Aaradhya. I could see you were hurt. Please tell me what's wrong.'
What came next, I wasn't ready for. *Ja na tu. Shivani ki care kar. Time waste mat kar apna.'*
It landed like a slap. My stomach sank. So it was about the watch. About Shivani.
I paused, collected myself, and typed slowly, each word weighted with the ache I carried: 'I know you're saying all this because of the watch. But Aaradhya—it's just a watch. Not an engagement ring. Not a secret code. Just a small gift she gave. She's just... a random person. And you? You're my world. Why does this small thing hurt us so much?'
Her reply was sharp, not yelling—but quieter in a way that made it worse.
'It's not about yelling. You say you love me, and you promised to keep your distance from her. Then what was all that? Shivani told me everything. Your "best friend," huh?'
Shivani told her? Why? What exactly did she say?

And Aaradhya didn't stop there. 'Weren't you both crossing a line? Was this the promise you made to me last birthday? *Or maybe it was me... who believed in you so easily.'*
That last line. *'Believed in you so easily.'*
It scorched, like friction on a burn. Like butter dropped into fire. And that fire came from a flicker—a harmless gift on my wrist.
I didn't know what to say. My thoughts twisted into knots. Finally, I sent: 'I'm sorry. Truly. If that hurts you, I won't ever wear that watch again. I'll keep my distance from Shivani. Just please... don't say you don't *believe* me. Don't throw us away like this.'
Tears welled up, but I blinked them back. My head throbbed. I typed, 'Just give me one chance. Please.'
Her response came like a rope thrown into deep water. 'Okay...' Then another. 'But I'm warning you—don't repeat this mistake again and again.'
It was a half-relief. A thin bandage on a deep cut. Too easy for her to say maybe—but I didn't blame her.
Still, my heart couldn't shift tracks so quickly. I was trying, but change isn't a switch you flick. It's something you grow into, painfully, slowly.
Didn't she take her time too? She hadn't fully come back yet—not the way she used to be. And here I was, still yearning, still breaking every day in silence just to see a glimpse of that old Aaradhya.

But if she could return, even a little... Then maybe I could change too.

In that pain I carried silently, I kept control of my emotions. Each morning, I'd find myself thrashing in bed, twisting in sheets that once knew peace, now drenched in longing—for her. It had become a ritual: wake, ache, repeat. Except for Diwali. That morning was different. No thrashing, no aching. I was already clutching my phone before I even opened my eyes. And there it was—her message.

'Happy Diwali, Dear' followed by a string of emojis—simple, but sweet enough to soften something within me.

I replied almost instantly, mirroring her words. She had also sent a photo of her home draped in fairy lights, shimmering softly like a dream that still had a heartbeat.

Later that day, Mumma made a *rangoli* and called me to help her. She always joked—half truth, half complaint—that she had no daughter, and so I had to fill the role. I smiled faintly, crouched beside her, and together we scattered colors into patterns. I clicked a photo of it and sent it to Aaradhya. A few moments later, she sent one of hers too.

Then evening arrived. The sky dipped into orange, and the sounds of fireworks—once magical—now felt like noise scratching the silence I had been trying to sit peacefully in. Aaradhya messaged again. A photo. Herself, in the very dress she bought the day she saw me wearing Shivani's watch. She looked beautiful—undeniably so.

'My beautiful lady,' I typed, trying to let her know I still saw her as the only light of my Diwali.

She responded with a smiling emoji. And then nothing.

She went offline. I waited. And then, as if right on cue, a message blinked in from Shivani: 'Happy Diwali Anuj!!'

The timing felt too deliberate, too exact—as if she had waited for Aaradhya to leave the stage before stepping into the light.

I replied quickly, dryly, 'Same to you', and locked my phone.

The screen continued to flash with her texts, one after the other, but I didn't open them. I wasn't in the mood for anyone else. I was waiting for Aaradhya. But she didn't come back.

The kurta I wore, the diyas that flickered, the crackers bursting outside—everything felt distant, dim.

And just like that, what should have been a night of celebration passed me by.

Like any other day. *Like a smile that never reached the eyes.*

A Farewell For You

As school resumed after Diwali, our classroom looked emptier than usual. Most were bunking to prepare for pre-boards. But Aaradhya came. Shivani too. And so did I.

It was about a week before the exams when the girls were practically begging our class teacher—Mehek ma'am—to spill the names of those nominated for the farewell awards. She didn't. Instead, she teased, 'This time your farewell will be right after pre-boards. Boys in proper suit-pants, girls in saree—no excuses.'

Everyone groaned, except me. I looked away, hiding a smile. I'll finally get to see her in a saree—in person. That single thought stuck with me more than the entire exam syllabus. I fast-forwarded the pre-boards in my head, all for that one day.

18 December 2024. A date I started dreaming about. No sooner had the pre-boards ended than the entire class broke

into full-on farewell fever. Discussions flew—what they'd wear, which awards they might get, whether their name would even be on the list.

I knew Aaradhya would be up there. Me? I wasn't sure. Vansh stood a chance too. But I didn't care about those awards. I only cared about the award—her smile, her glance, her standing beside me—that kind of win.
We were ordered to shave every last trace of facial hair. Not even a hint of stubble allowed. I stared at my reflection, hesitant. Weeks of effort—gone in seconds.
Black was banned too, so I wore the blue suit. The same one I secretly hoped would match something on her.

I reached the general bus stop by 5:20. Everyone was already there—Ashwin, Aarohi, Vansh, some tenth graders... and her. Aaradhya.
Sky blue saree. The same colour from Diwali 2023. I'd seen it back then in a photo. But today, in person—she was ethereal. Offline had a different magic.

We stood in groups, chatting loosely. I found myself next to her. *'Kya baat hai bhai,'* Vansh smirked, glancing between us and making an ok symbol. Aarohi leaned close and whispered, *'Match karke pehne ho na?'* I blushed. 'Nope. Just a coincidence.' Aaradhya was blushing too. And in that moment—coincidence or not—it felt like something hopeful was aligning.

The bus finally arrived. Atif's and Shreya's groups were already there, along with Mehek ma'am. We climbed in, aiming for the back seats—me, Ashwin, and Vansh claimed one row; Aaradhya, Aarohi, and Shreya took the one ahead.

The bus buzzed with chatter and laughter. I, though, just sat there—quiet, eyes locked on her. Her voice, her soft laugh, the way she held that handkerchief like she always did. Same grace. Same charm.
And somehow, even from a seat behind, she felt impossibly far and achingly close, all at once.

But soon, I drifted back into the fun—the most amusing part was watching her, Aaradhya, being amazed by everything like a little child in wonderland.

And just like that, we reached the Raipur school. From the bus window, I could already spot a sea of students out there. They laughed, chatted, and posed for selfies.

Among them, someone familiar stood out—Harsh, my classmate from early primary days. He had studied with us till 9th before transferring here. We exchanged greetings; he looked so different now—older, sharper, as if time had rushed ahead for him.

Barely had we formed lines to move to our assigned rooms when Shivani found me. She instantly started filling my ears, demanding compliments—her outfit, her look, everything. I smiled awkwardly, trying not to look too long.

I had Shivani's watch in my bag—but I wasn't going to wear it. Aaradhya had told me not to, and I wasn't going to risk it.

I stayed mostly with the boys. Arun dragged me along wherever he went until breakfast was served. After that, we entered their massive school hall, decorated for the farewell program. A large sound system was set up, and the hall itself—it was at least three times the size of ours.
We were directed to our seats: 12th graders on the right, 10th on the left. I sat next to Vansh; Aaradhya was right in front of me, to the side, and strangers sat behind and beside us.
The program struggled to begin—teachers trying to assemble the restless students, a choir that couldn't get synced, and the heat making everyone grumpy. We waited nearly 50 minutes before things finally started.
After the prayer session, the crowd stood and clapped as our special guest entered—Snehal Pinto.
Next was the worship song segment. We were dragged into an hour of forced dancing—no couple steps, no cool grooves, just moving hands and swaying bodies. The singers were good, but the dancing felt dry. Most did it out of fear, some out of habit. Strangely enough, Arun gave it his all, and even earned a special mention from Snehal Pinto himself.

Next came the welcome songs and speeches. Kunal leaned over and joked, 'English or Spanish?' as we watched a group of 11th grade girls deliver a welcome speech—first in Spanish, then translated in English. It felt more like a flex than a formality.

Then Snehal Pinto took the stage for a long speech. She invited a few students to come up and share their experiences and future plans. Most of them stumbled through, barely able to hold the mic properly. Our branch's students clearly stood out—even our 10th graders were more confident than theirs.

The program moved ahead, and finally came the moment everyone had been waiting for: the award ceremony.

First came our school's turn. Four students from 10th were called up first, all smiles and excitement. Then it was the 12th grade—our batch.

They began with individual recognitions. Vartika was called for the Excellence in Academics Award, and the crowd applauded hard. Then Rehan got the Excellence in International Events Award, and cheers followed again. And then—unexpectedly—my name echoed through the mic.

I froze for a second. Was it really me? I stood up slowly, a smile forming on my face. Vansh shouted my name from the back, the girls cheered, and the applause felt endless. As I walked toward the stage, it felt like a dream.

'Outstanding All Rounder Award', Snehal Pinto Ma'am announced.

All Rounder? I thought. For what exactly? I didn't know. But I was happy. Maybe someone did notice something in me.

Then came the most awaited moment: the Xavier's Princess Award. And it went to none other than—Aaradhya.

My heart bloomed. She looked radiant, her saree flowing perfectly, now crowned with a sparkling tiara and a graceful sash. I couldn't stop smiling. That moment—her smile, the spotlight—it felt perfect. But the feeling didn't last long.

The next announcement: Xavier's Prince. It was Vansh.

I clapped, I smiled, but a dull ache pinched somewhere. *I wanted to stand beside her—not just in photos, but in that moment, in that title.* Still, I was happy for him. He deserved it.

They were crowned together, the perfect Prince and Princess. But not the perfect match.

Photos followed—group shots, class shots, individual ones with ma'am and principal.

Aaradhya and I smiled at each other from a distance. Just that. A moment. And the camera clicked.

As we stepped down from the stage, Vansh and Aaradhya were asked to stay back. The other branches exited first, and then all the Princes and Princesses from different schools were called up again—to cut the cake.

I returned to my seat. When I looked at Aarohi, her face mirrored mine—blank, strained, somewhere between a smile and a sigh. Maybe she felt it too. That strange ache. That's when the thought hit me—*I often called Aarohi and myself the South Poles of a magnet. While Vansh and Aaradhya? The North Poles.*
Aaradhya was my love. Vansh, my best friend. Two North Poles being attracted by the South. Aarohi? Aaradhya's best friend. And Vansh? The one she loved. Again North Poles attracted to the South.
We South Poles didn't attract each other. We just co-existed. Fought. Disagreed. And yet, in this moment, we were sitting with the same emotion—watching the ones we loved from a distance.

Vansh and Aaradhya returned, laughing softly as they walked back. They sat beside us again. Aarohi congratulated Aaradhya, and I nodded to Vansh.
Then, as they sat down, both removed their sashes and crowns. Aaradhya smiled faintly and said,
'If my love isn't the Prince, I don't accept being the Princess.'
Vansh echoed the same.
It felt sweet, loyal—like a silent confession—but also incomplete. Because some words soothe, but never heal. Some truths stab even when wrapped in affection.

I kept a smile on my face. A forced one.

Because **sometimes, it's easier to hide pain than to explain it.**

The program went on with the vote of thanks, a closing chorus, and finally, the school anthems followed by the national anthem.

After that, everything turned into a frenzy—students rushing to Snehal Pinto ma'am for selfies, loud Bollywood music blasting from the speakers, groups forming and dancing without a care. And me? I just sat there. Staring at the trophy in my hand. Which felt meaningless now.

Shivani was the first who noticed my state. She walked up, cheerful as always, *'chal, dance karenge! Akele kyu baitha hai?'* I didn't respond.

She sat beside me. *'Kya hua yaar? Itna sad kyun hai?'*

Then she looked at the trophy. *'Tujhe Prince banna tha na?'*

I was shocked. How did she know? Did she know about me and Aaradhya? But then she smiled and said,

'Koi nahi. All Rounder bhi toh kafi achha hai. Aur waise... even if you didn't become the Prince, you'll always be my Prince.'

And that—that was too much. Too direct. Too assumptive. She grabbed my arm and pulled me toward the crowd. Aaradhya caught sight of us. Her face fell and in the next second, she turned and walked away. Why? Why can't anything ever just be okay? Aarohi followed Aaradhya.

I stood there, lost, confused. Shivani asked, 'What's wrong?'

I muttered, 'Nothing.'

'Toh dance kar.'

'I'm not in the mood,' I said—and walked away, fast, almost
running—straight to the washroom.
And before I even made it inside, the tears came. I hid my
face with my hands, washing it again and again.
'Why does this always happen to me?' I whispered. 'Why am
I so unlucky?'
I splashed water on my face again. Just then, a few 10th
graders of Ryan Raipur walked in. I pretended I was fine,
just here to pee.
As they left, more tears poured.
Heavier and true. And I stood there, drenched in silence and
lost in timelessness.

And if everything that had already happened that day wasn't
enough, one more thing had to add to it.

After I was drained from all the crying, we went for lunch.
Vansh had already sensed something was wrong. But it was
Aarohi who walked over and bluntly told me, *'Tune uska
pura makeup kharab kar diya!'*
I stared, confused.too *'Vo ro rahi thi,'* she added quietly.
And just like that, the pain hit again, sharp and instant, I
could burst into tears anytime.
'Usko misunderstanding ho gayi hai, yaar...' I muttered,
helplessly trying to explain everything—how Shivani
dragged me, how I didn't want any of that. Aarohi listened
and said she'd try to talk to Aaradhya. I hoped it would
work. But some things just don't unfold the way we wish.

On the way back in the bus, all of us—Aaradhya, Vansh, Aarohi, Ashwin, and I—sat together in the last row. At first, Vansh sat between me and Aaradhya, but then, out of nowhere, he smiled and forcefully switched seats with me. It left both of us sitting side by side. She didn't say much. Her silence was heavy, still upset from earlier. Aarohi, thankfully, tried to get her to talk, and eventually she did—just a little.

We played songs on one phone, and vibed together. It could've been such a happy ride back, if only she hadn't been so distant. I didn't know what else to do.
Once everyone got off, only Vansh and I were left on the bus. If the usual route had been followed, it would've been Aaradhya and me instead.

I told him everything. Shivani. The award moment. The misunderstanding.
He listened, nodded. But what could he really do? Some things weren't fixable by a friend. He stepped off the bus. And then, quietly, I did too.

I had tried explaining everything to her on Instagram, again and again—but she wouldn't hear me out.

Instead, she'd say that she never expected this from me, that her fear had been right all along—*'Familiarity breeds contempt.'*

Each word felt like an arrow, hitting exactly where it hurt most. But even after everything, I still went to her. No matter how much she cried, accused, or overthought, I kept trying. And I cried too—enough to fill a dried lake.
But she wasn't ready to hear me. Wasn't ready to *believe* me. Not even for a second. And when I explained it all one last time—with all the desperation, frustration, and helplessness bottled inside—it came out brutally raw.
And finally, she said, *'Koi baat nahi.'*
But I knew. I knew she hadn't really forgiven me.
She was still under the shadow of that hurt.
And maybe it wasn't even my fault. Maybe it wasn't hers either. Still, I said sorry. She started talking normally after that. But deep down, I could see it in her texts—she still wasn't okay.

"Welcome Back"

And just like that, the final days of 2024 passed—drenched in the same quiet despair. No new achievements. And the few things I had built in the last year? Lost. Like sand slipping through fingers I never closed tightly enough.

Where did I go wrong?

I asked myself that on the night of December 31st. Aaradhya had started talking again, sure—but only just enough to keep things from falling apart completely. There was no warmth, no softness, no trace of what we used to be. She was trying not to hurt me, maybe, but I could feel it—she wasn't okay. And still, I kept hoping. Kept expecting. Kept failing.
What stung worse was how she'd reacted to Shivani. The jealousy, the accusations—it almost felt like she still cared. But did she? Or was it just wounded pride?

Whatever it was, I clung to it like a fool. And quietly, I promised myself—and her, in some invisible language we'd forgotten how to speak—that I'd never choose another girl. Never.

It was 11:57 p.m. and the new year was just three minutes away. My mind was a mess. Another year wasted. Another chance I hadn't taken. I told myself 2025 had to be better—studies, discipline, everything in control. But those promises felt empty, like scribbles on fogged glass. And somehow, something else felt more urgent than even that. I was staring at my phone, eyes dry, mind on fire—waiting to wish Aaradhya at exactly 12:00. Last year, I'd messaged her first. This time, I wanted to see if she'd take the lead. Just once. Just this year. Maybe then I'd know—if I still meant something. Maybe I already knew I was setting myself up for disappointment. But some hopes are cruel that way. Midnight struck. A notification appeared on my lock screen—Shivani.
'Happy New Year.'
I didn't open it. I didn't even blink. Because it wasn't the message I was waiting for. I waited... and waited. Nothing. Sleep crept in like betrayal—I hadn't planned to fall asleep, but I did. Slumped on the chair, head resting on the cold table. The last time I remember checking the screen, it was 1 a.m. Still nothing from her. Still silence.

I let myself believe that maybe she slept early. Maybe she forgot. Maybe she didn't mean anything by it.

I forgave her quietly. Even when a part of me was breaking apart. Next morning—before brushing, before even opening the curtains—I checked WhatsApp. And there it was. Aaradhya's message.

'Happy new year dear... I know you're busy with your new friend Shivani so you didn't have much time to wish me even a happy new year. But I have time for you, so I did. I saw you both were online till 1 a.m... maybe chatting with each other!'

Every word felt like a slap. Not because she was wrong—but because she didn't even try to ask. Didn't even care to hear my side. Just conclusions. Judgments. Like always.

I didn't reply to her because I knew she wouldn't understand. It just made the silence thicker and more bitter.

Eventually, I opened Shivani's message. It read like a poem.

'Happy New Year, my dearest friend.

Another chapter begins, and I'm so grateful you're still part of my story.

You've seen me at my worst, and never let go of my hand...'

The rest blurred. I didn't need to read it all. I already knew it.

I replied, 'I know this message. It's from ChatGPT. I saw it there last night. You're sending me this?'

The irony almost made me laugh. Almost, but I didn't.

How could I be laughing in that kind of situation?

She replied instantly, even though she'd been offline.
'I don't have poetic qualities... that's why I took help, sorry.'
I should've left it there. But I didn't. I typed again,
mechanically: 'What matters is emotion. Language is just a
tool. And you tried. So thanks. And... there's no sorry in
friendship, *itna formality kyu dikhana?*'
She replied with a smiley and heart emoji. A heart.
Then she added: *'This heart symbolises our friendship.'*
I stared at the screen. But I didn't feel anything.
No comfort. No peace. No sense of being cared for.
Only one thought stuck in my mind like a thorn:
Why wasn't it Aaradhya? And why did it feel like she never
would be again?

I talked to Vansh about it the next day. About how she
didn't even stop to think—not for a second—before
accusing me. How I'd stayed up so long, just waiting for her,
hoping she'd care enough to text first. And still, she assumed
the worst. As always, Vansh said he'd handle it. And he did. I
started noticing the signs soon enough.

No, this year hadn't begun like the last one did—with
midnight wishes and warmth. But somewhere in the
wreckage of that night, I held on to something small,
something stubborn—Hope.
Hope that maybe, somehow, things might find a way back
to what they used to be—or become something better. And

that hope—however small—was enough to initiate
something.
It was the last day of January 2025. Aaradhya's birthday.
The moment I woke up, I messaged her. A simple birthday
wish. Nothing dramatic—just an attempt to leave the past
behind. By then, I'd convinced myself that I had moved on.
Maybe she had too.

When I saw her on the bus, she was smiling—but not like
before. The charm she carried on her last birthday... it wasn't
there. It was dull, distant. I figured she must've seen my
message. Maybe she remembered how I hadn't wished her
last year. Maybe she still hadn't forgiven that.
Later, in school, she and Shivani were distributing
chocolates. But I wasn't there. Neither was Shaurya. Jitesh
sir had pulled us aside for some random
responsibility—assigning roles to juniors for an event.
She entered the room, gave sir a chocolate, and even handed
one to Shaurya. But when her eyes met mine—nothing. She
looked away. Quietly slipped out.
I heard Shivani whispering behind her, *'Usse kyun nahi
diya?'*
Aaradhya's voice was low but sharp. *'Ja tu de de.'*
And so Shivani walked up to me, that single candy in her
hand. I refused.

'Usse nahi dena tha to main kyun loon?' I said.

She didn't reply. Just dropped it in my pocket and walked away.
The silence she left behind burned louder than words.
As soon as she left, I pulled the chocolate out and gave it to a small second-grader. It was childish, maybe, but the gesture had stung. Why couldn't she just give it herself?
A tension rose in my chest—but it shattered a little later. Just briefly.

On the way back, the bus buzzed with chatter. That's when Aaradhya walked over, quietly, and handed me a small box of Ferrero Rocher. No words, just a smile.
She respected what I said earlier regarding chocolates. She tried. And I saw that. I smiled back, softly wished her happy birthday again. For a fleeting moment, it felt like something was coming back together. Like the distance between us was melting.
But peace doesn't last for me. Not even for a second.
Ashwin's voice cut through everything. *'Subah se wish nahi kiya, ab chocolate mil raha hai to kar raha hai.'*
And Aaradhya—she didn't defend me.
She just let out a 'hmph' and said, *'Kya kar sakte hai... kuch log hote hai... besharam.'*
It hit harder than it should've. I looked down, didn't say a word. Just took the box and stuffed it deep into my bag. I wasn't sure if I was more hurt by what she said—or by how quickly that little moment of hope had vanished again.

At home, something finally felt a little better.

Aaradhya had called me after a long time, she sounded a bit
tensed asaid sorry—for what she'd said on the bus. She'd
seen my birthday wish later and realized I had wished her
early in the morning. Maybe, this time, her apology was real.
Maybe she meant it.
But I couldn't keep it all inside. So I asked, why didn't you
give me the chocolate yourself? Why did Shivani have to do
it?
She hesitated, then replied with something I hadn't
expected.
'Because Shivani was with me... and she has feelings for you.
She told me everything. She didn't know about us. That's
why she was... like that. It was unintentional. She's a good
person. If she'd known, maybe she wouldn't have even tried
looking at you that way.' So that was it.
The way Shivani behaved, the signs I'd brushed off—they all
made sense now. She had been loving me silently. I had a
feeling, but now it was confirmed.
Aaradhya's voice softened. 'And I'm sorry. For the
accusations. I misunderstood everything. And when I
realized that... when I saw your message... I knew I'd hurt
you. I just hope you can forgive me.'
I took a breath. Then said, 'So you finally understand it
wasn't my fault. And there's no need to carry guilt for it.
Don't you remember what I told you on 16th October,

2023? That *no matter how much wrong you do, just come to me—and I'll forgive you every time. Because I love you.*'
She went silent for a moment and then she said it.
'I love you too.'
And in that moment, everything came rushing back. All the memories, the laughter, the pain, the promises. It felt like we had finally come back to the version of us we were always meant to be.
But before I could sink into the comfort of it, she added, 'That's good... but who said you didn't have a fault?'
It hit like a sharp stone in still water.
'What fault?' I asked, my fingers cold suddenly.
Her reply came fast, too fast: 'It was your fault because you should've avoided her. No matter what. *If you really love someone, you can hurt anyone for them.*'
Two emotions crashed inside me—one of love, the other of guilt. But I couldn't lose her again.
Especially when she continued, with her tone gentler now. *'You don't need to put in excess effort to reach me. If it's meant to happen, it will. And you already have—put in all the necessary efforts. What's missing now is just... patience.* Wait for me. I promise, once things settle down, I'll be the one accusing you of not meeting me enough.'

My heart swelled. Her feelings were still there—still alive, still strong. I promised her, 'I will. I'll preserve all my love. Just for you. All your precious demands—duly noted.'

And that day... that day felt like the most beautiful day of the year. *Like sunlight after a long winter.* Her words stayed with me—not as echoes of pain, but as quiet proof that love had survived everything. For the first time in months, my heart felt calm. Everything wasn't perfect, but it was ours again. And that was enough.

Final Misunderstanding

And then, with that happiness, I fought through the board exams. Aaradhya was far more present than she'd been in those earlier, dreadful days—at least on the screen of my phone. I waited for her, believed in her, trusted that she'd come back fully. And with that mindset, the boards ended. Away from distractions like Shivani, I stayed focused on her. Strangely, Shivani—despite all the mess—had unknowingly played her part in weaving us back together. And Vansh, as always, remained the thread that kept us from falling apart. Aaradhya kept her promise. We met again—a week after the final exam. But this time, it was for a different reason.

On 10th April, the entire class met at school—finally free from the weight of board exams. It was a casual reunion, the kind that didn't need structure—just a shared desire to be together once more, unsure of when we'd meet again. Aaradhya, Shivani, and Aarohi were with the girls around Jitesh Sir, while I stood with Vansh, Shaurya, and the others, finalizing the plan for our outing to Surya Treasure Island Mall.

When I asked, *Jo nahi aaye hain unko kaise bataoge?'*, Arun replied casually, *'Kaun nahi aaya hai? Kunal ko text kar dena, aur Ashwin jaise jo hamesha bahana banate hain unko batane ki zarurat nahi.'* I pulled out my phone to text Kunal, but just then, I caught a glimpse of Shivani sneaking away from the group of girls, eyeing our side. I pretended not to notice and placed my phone on the table, just as Mehek Ma'am called me to the staff room—she'd found a certificate I'd left behind.

When I returned, everyone had already started heading to the chemistry lab. That's when Shivani came up and asked where we were going. I was about to answer when Vansh suddenly covered my mouth and pulled me away. All Shivani could say behind us was, *'Arey yaar...'*

Once we were a few steps away, Vansh handed me my phone and said bluntly, *'Abhi tera phone check kar rahi thi.'* I blinked. 'Oh? Why?' I asked. He frowned, *'Pata nahi. Par usne mujhse bhi pucha tha ki hum kahan ja rahe hain. Maine bola tujhe kya, tu Anuj se door rahe to hi accha hai. Fir boli, maine kuch kiya kya,* did I hurt him? *Gussa hai kya?* When I said that I don't know, she said that *kaisa dost hai re tu, tujhe kuch pata hi nahi hota uske baare mein, mujhe itna gussa aaya na ki mai uspe chilla diya ki nikal yaha se* after that just moments later, I saw her with your phone—Kunal's chat open. I snatched it back and shouted at her—*Badtameez, uska phone kaise li tu?* And then she said, *mujhe laga call aa raha tha* and ran off.'

I quickly checked Kunal's chat—only the meet location and time were open. if she'd seen that, she wouldn't have needed to ask me where we were going, so if practically felt alright. I felt a strange relief—but also a chill. Some lines had been crossed and some even got broken. *'Tu door hi rehna uss aurat se,'* Vansh said in an angrier tone.

When I reached home, Aaradhya's message lit up my screen: 'There are so many things I want to tell you. I'm too excited. You're busy tonight, and I might not be available tomorrow, so let's meet the day after—promise me.' And I did. I promised. My heart was light—giddy, even. All those days of silent hope, unreturned texts, and restless tears suddenly felt worth it. She was waiting too. Her excitement sparked mine, and for the first time in a long while, the future didn't feel uncertain. It felt warm.

And in that warmth, I readied myself for the meet—black T-shirt on, paired with a smart trouser for that clean, aesthetic look. Since Vansh had gone to pick up Arun, I had to come alone. I got on the scooty, heart racing and a smile on my face, the kind that Aaradhya's excitement had gifted me.

I reached the mall parking and just as I parked, Vansh called. I answered, telling him I was in the parking lot. That's when Shivani's call came through. I hadn't even reacted when Vansh, overhearing, snapped, '*Mat pick kar. Aaja. Mat baat karna uss se.*' I nodded and ignored the call.

Inside, everyone had already gathered, laughter floating in the air. Like the last time, there wasn't a fixed plan until Shaurya announced, '*Pehle game, fir ghumna, fir khana, fir ghar,*' and surprisingly, it got unanimous approval. After the arcade session, Vansh and I went to get ice cream. Shivani's call flashed again. Vansh repeated with more force, '*Block kar de usse.*' I chuckled awkwardly, waving it off, just as I realized I had forgotten my wallet in the scooty.

I rushed to get it, only to return and find Vansh had already paid. But before I could thank him, he turned toward me, expression dark, and growled, '*Bey!*' Confused, I asked what happened. He grabbed my shoulder and turned me around—and there she was. Shivani.
'*Mai bola tha usse baat mat kar, aur tu usse le aya?*' Vansh asked.
'*Hain? Mai nahi laya usse! Mujhe kya pata kaha se aa gayi,*' I defended, equally stunned.
He stormed toward her. '*Anuj ka picha karte karte yaha aa gayi?*' he snapped.

Shivani, feigning surprise, lifted a shopping bag. *'Nahin toh! Main toh yahi thi*, birthday shopping.'
Vansh didn't buy it. 'You're lying.'
'See, shopping stuff!' she insisted.
Without another word, Vansh grabbed my hand and walked off toward the arcade crowd, tossing a final line over his shoulder—*'Ja ja, shopping kar.'*
After dragging me into the crowd, Vansh said sharply, *'Vo jhooth bol rahi hai! Pakka! Dur hi rehna. Agar Aaradhya ko pata chala toh—'*
I tried to calm him down, *'Chinta mat kar, nahi jaunga. Aur waise bhi, Aaradhya isn't here, she won't get to know.'*
He snapped back, *'Vo nahi hai matlab karega!?'*
I chuckled, brushing it off. *'Nah.'*

Later, we all reached Zudio and went upstairs to the men's section, while Shivani headed to the women's floor below. Most of the boys got busy at the perfume counter. Shaurya and I were flipping through shirts when Shivani called me from the stairs.
'Mere sath koi nahi aaya, samajh nahi aa raha kya achha hai kya nahi... bta de na.'
I turned to Shaurya, 'I'll be back in a bit. If I don't, don't wait.'
She was alone. I thought helping her out would be quick. She tried outfit after outfit—yellow, pink gown, a black saree somewhere else. I barely commented; I had no clue about this stuff. If it were Aaradhya, maybe I would've known

what to say. Eventually, she settled on something she liked, and I assumed I was done.

But just as I was heading back, she pulled me again.

'Ab kya hua?' I asked.

'Jhumke to bata de yaar.'

'I don't know about these things! *Mujhe pyas lag rahi hai,* and the guys are waiting.'

'Pyaas lag rahi hai? Come.'

She bought me a hot chocolate. I took a sip and turned to go when she stopped me again. *'Arey, kaha ja raha hai? Maine tujhe hot chocolate dilaya na, badle mein bta to de kaunsa accha hai!'*

With a sigh, I stayed, giving half-hearted 'hmm's to whatever she showed. I was bored. Then I caught a glimpse of Vansh staring down from the upper floor—his expression said everything. He looked away angrily. I panicked, was he angry?

'I need to go,' I told Shivani and rushed upstairs.

'Sorry, mai late ho gaya,' I said to Vansh.

He didn't respond. When he finally did, it stung:

'Ja na tu. Reh ussi ke saath.'

That silence over the meal was heavier than the burger in my hand. No one else noticed it much, but I did. I tried explaining to the group, *'Humara kuch nahi hai na bhai, bas usse kuch puchna tha.'* But Vansh stayed cold.

We all got home. I messaged him—no reply. Just seen marks. And it felt worse than anything Shivani could've ever done.

And what felt even worse than Vansh's silence—something that hit deeper—was what came next.

That evening, clouds gathered like a quiet warning. The wind grew restless, and a light drizzle tapped against the windows when my phone buzzed with a message I didn't expect.

Aaradhya: 'Anuj. Come to the badminton court. I want to meet you!'

It was sudden. 'Weren't you going somewhere?' I replied, surprised.

She shot back, *'Ye kaam zyada zaruri hai!'* with a tense emoji.

'Kuch hua hai kya?' I typed, a bit uneasy.

'Tu bas aa jaldi!' she insisted, dropping an angry emoji this time.

I didn't push further. Just sent an 'okay' and watched her go offline.

It was raining. And I had no idea what could be so urgent. But I knew one thing—this wasn't like any of our usual meets. Something had changed. By the time I reached, it was dark, a new moon night. When I returned with my eyes full of tears.

I was back at the last page of my diary, the shayari, I had written that night. It kept reminding of that one scene again and again: *'He might've said something, but believe me-'*
—*'I don't believe you!'*
Tears welled up before I could stop them. No matter how much I tried, those four words wouldn't leave me alone—**'I Don't *Believe* You!'**

"I Don't Believe You"

—Aditya Chauhan and Shashank Mishra

With that final line, I closed my old diary, once again completing to narrate our story to Aaradhya.
'Kitna roya tha na main uss din,' I said with a soft chuckle.

Aaradhya handed me a cup of tea, her smile as calm as the evening breeze. 'But then everything went alright,' she said, taking her seat beside me.

'Yeah,' I nodded, taking a sip. *'Vo to hona hi tha.'*

The front door creaked open—Anya was back from school. She rushed in, tossed her bag onto the sofa, and hugged Aaradhya tight.
'Mummy!' she giggled.
'How was your day?' Aaradhya asked.
'Cool!' Anya chirped before darting off to freshen up.

I smiled, watching them. 'It really feels like a dream... after everything, after all those days when we didn't know where we were headed—we're here. Together.'

Aaradhya stood, brushing her hair behind her ear. 'But if you hadn't accepted your fault and apologized...'
'And if you hadn't forgiven me,' I added quietly.
We both paused—then, in perfect unison, we said:
'We wouldn't have been together.'

Sometimes, even a misunderstanding becomes a conflict you couldn't win.
But love... love isn't about sitting still and watching the threads of your relationship tear apart.

It takes nothing more than losing the one you love
for your lost soul to beg to leave the body it no longer feels at home in.
It takes nothing more than that loss to turn lovers into strangers—
or something even more treacherous... grieving what could've been.

But it also takes nothing more than one word—sorry—to stop it.

And if your love is truly real,
and if their love still lingers, even after all you've been through,
they'll let go of ego, and forgive you,
even after saying, ***"I Don't Believe You."***